THE SUNSET SOVEREIGN

A DRAGON'S MEMOIR

Copyright © 2024 by Laura Huie

All rights reserved. No part of this publication may be reproduced, distributed, or transmitted in any form or by any means, including photocopying, recording, or other electronic or mechanical methods, without the prior written permission of the publisher, except as permitted by U.S. copyright law. It is illegal to copy this book, post it to a website, or distribute it by any other means without permission.

The story, all names, characters, and incidents portrayed in this production are fictitious. No identification with actual persons (living or deceased), places, buildings, and products is intended or should be inferred.

Typography by Jay Wolf (https://jayxwolf.carrd.co/)

Typesetting by Konstance (https://linktr.ee/konstancek)

Cover art from Warm_Tail (https://www.shutterstock.com/g/WarmTail)

Quacks A Lot Publishing First hardcover edition November 2024

ISBN 979-8-218-53437-0

To the one who loved this color and
wanted the story of a dragon.

To the one who motivated me to push
myself and grow as a writer.

Both of you are always telling
me to rest. Thank you.

To the Inkfort Press staff, thank
you for this adventure.

CONTENTS

1. THE HUNT

The gold coins with the engraved heads of lords, kings, queens, or creatures of old and long forgotten were in piles and covered in dirt. Swords of monster hunters lay abandoned in their sheaths or ruined from being stepped on. Hollow armor laid about with the bones turned to dust. Piles of fortune that could have saved the nation during times of struggle laid covered in dirt and abandoned with time.

Sisal had not burst into flames yet; her soul was pure enough to enter the cave. Now she needed to be adequately light-footed to stalk her target.

The deep breath of the monster exhaled out, the smell of sulfur heavy in the air. Sisal held her breath to prevent coughing. She had to get a stealth attack to have any sort of advantage in this fight. She would finally free their nation from this fabled beast. It all started with her creeping into the cave and sliding along the wall. Fifty-fifty odds on which way to go, and she chose the wrong side of the first cavern. Across all the dried-up stalactites and stalagmites, a closed, deep blue stone door sat on the other side of the cave, way too small for the monster to go through. It was too late to move. The creature was coming out of the archway that led to another cavern in the back.

She spent weeks researching and spent all her gold to prepare for this mission the Guild Adventures gave her. The rumor of "Bare yourself to the Beast to receive what you seek" was the reason she equipped herself with light leather armor and gear. She had to stay fast enough to avoid the beast's breath, their claws, their tail, and the very sharp teeth, none of which her armor could stop. A dragon could be quick, but its size did not make it as agile as her, especially this early before sunrise. The beast was still sleeping.

She gasped out the breath she held on to, instantly covering her mouth in regret. The rhythmic sound of the monster's breath stopped. The floor shook beneath her feet as the fabled beast moved. Eyes darting around, she looked for shelter and dived behind a statue of a burnt red dragon. Quickly, she tightened her bowstring, two arrows strung on it. Her grandfather found a dragon scale out near the Black Forest when he was a kid. He gave it to her so she could fill her quiver with dragon scale arrowheads.

The ground shook more when the creature entered the wide, gold-filled chamber. Research mentioned a weak point on the back of her target, and worse case she knew of one more, the eyes. They were always the weak point on any creature, like the yeti she killed.

The ground stilled. She peeked through the underside of the dragon statue, where pigment dark red flakes fell off. The target's stature was large. She knew it was big, but seeing something the size of the palace saunter into the first cavern put a different meaning to the word big. It made the dragon statue look like a miniature meant for child's play. The empty chamber suddenly felt too inadequate to hold such a mythical sized creature. Smoke stacks sprawled out of its nostrils as its head twisted around, looking. Its dark brown claws glistened, the dark red scales giving it a strong armor against a simple dagger attack. The wings were darker than the rest of it, tucked in at its sides. If only she had remained quiet earlier, she could have set up the explosives on the ceiling, but now she had to go with a different plan. A few stalagmites had their tops flattened and with ceramics displaying the dragon were everywhere, more places she could hide in a fight. Quickly she ducked her head as the monster's golden eyes looked low, pausing at the statue for a moment, before

turning around and going back to its chamber.

The long-spiked tail swung back and forth. Strong plates, some as thick as tree trunks, ran up its back. But one was missing, leaving a narrow pink scar. Narrow when compared to the size of the dragon, something Sisal could shoot and hit. Research said freeze spells were the dragon's weakness. From her bag, she pulled out the ice spell into her arrowheads. The spell would last only an hour, but all fights with any monster were over in ten minutes. In order to get a clear shot, she moved out from her hiding position, careful to avoid stepping into the gold coins, pulled the string taut and launched the arrows.

They hissed through the air, a white streak of frosted air following their path. The noise was too loud, and the dragon paused and turned too slowly. The frosted arrows hit its backside. Cracking blue-white ice spread out over the dragon's back near the exposed area. The beast roared in pain upward into the roof of the cavern. It let out a hot breath and shook the ceiling. Shards of stone fell down on the piles of gold coins. Sisal chased after the iced over area on the dragon. She had to get another hit in to cause critical damage. An injury on the back of the beast would give her the upper hand needed in this fight. She was a human facing a dragon larger than the palace of Vakfored. This was like a fight between a beetle taking on the kitchen cat. She grabbed another iced dragon arrowhead, pulled it back, and shot into the beast's iced up back. A deafening roar erupted from the beast. Her ears rung and the surrounding environment shook, threating to trip her. All of it was a distraction from the attack of the monster's tail that swatted her into a pile of coins. The gold coins scattered about as she took in a deep breath and rolled out of the way before another smack down from the jasper tail nearby. The currency glistened like glitter off the beast's tail.

Sisal grabbed for her bow but came up empty-handed. Her eyes darted around, trying to find a solution, but in this ancient cavern, any bows that had lasted this long would have snapped, and she had no string available. Throwing dragon pottery at her target would do nothing. There

were no more long-distance options. She drew her sword from the sheath as the next best thing. Sword out, and she snapped her wrist to call upon the magical shield hiding in her bracelet. It could survive three hits. The shop owner said it could even stop magical attacks. She spent every coin on equipment for this mission.

Four very short inhaled breaths came from the dragon, its tail slithering around. It rolled its shoulders, threatening to stretch out its wings.

"It's been a long time since I've felt physical pain."

The voice resonated power that she felt in her bones. Its mouth stretched open, revealing the large jagged teeth. Many heroes and warriors had died inside its mouth. Sisal knew she would not be the next one. She was ready with her Iridium dwarven crafted sword, honed to withstand any fire attack. The King himself gifted the sword to her once she accepted this mission, the ruby in it to match her ferocity and hair. Since the day she could walk, she constantly had to prove herself to others that she would be strong enough to do this mission. Now, she had the equipment to stop the monster that threatened Vakfored, her home.

Grabbing at a small pouch of dust in her pocket, she threw the purple powder up in the air and ran through it. The chrome and mushroom smell covered her. For the next twenty seconds, she would be invisible to the beast. A trick she used before on the yeti monster, but a dragon was a different game.

Its eyes, the color of its hoard, narrowed and looked around. "Little human, that's very clever of you."

Sisal knew she couldn't stay still and ran toward the belly of the dragon. It took eight seconds to get there. Some of its scales were as tall as her, while others were only as big as her abdomen. No wonder it only took one scale to make all the arrowheads. The tail swung at the gold pile where Sisal visibly stood last. She remained underneath the stomach, staying light on her feet as she looked for the gap in its scales where she could cut it. Rumors mentioned an injury near its heart. Being next to the dragon, it was easy to predict all its movement.

Except for a forward charge. It was unfair that a creature so large could still move so explosive suddenly. As the beast ran forward, it swung its tail like a hunting hound finding the scent of prey. She tried to stay on the underside, near the middle. Her stride was too small compared to the monster. Its tail scraped up against her, knocking her over. The invisibility dust was no longer on her, and she used up one hit of her shield. Facing such an intelligent beast over a millennium old, it was a fool's dream to think some simple tricks would outsmart it. But even the most intelligent person falls for the simple shoulder tap joke. She tossed more dust into the air, but instead of running to the beast, she slowed her walk. Stepping lightly around the jewels, pottery, and garland covered stalagmites. Finally, she arrived at a small alcove in the wall, still too far from the door she originally sought, but the powder would end soon.

The dragon sighed, smoke dissipating out of its mouth. It lowered its head, chuckling. Large rings wafted out and then a stream of smoke filled the low area. It was going to smoke her out. Its golden eyes were still towered above her, out of reach of her sword even with the beast's head on the ground. The fire tongues coming from its mouth illuminated its eyes. The smoke grew and tendrils reached out to her.

Gingerly, she reached down and grabbed a handful of gems and coins. These coins just had a simple sketching with an outline of dragon wings on them. The dragon statue, coins, and even the pot next to her had images of a dragon on it. With all the coins here, she actually could count the size of its ego. She threw the coins and gems at a clay pot standing on a pedestal with glowing orbs wrapped around it. It tipped over, and it fell down onto the pile of coins nearby. The dragon flung around and swung a giant claw toward the pot. The back of the stubby leg created a chance for her to run up it and charge toward the golden target, its eye.

Sprinting up the scales of a dragon was easier than she had expected, as long as she landed right where the ridges were. The metal of her sword glistened icy blue, magic sizzling along as it charged the attack to pierce the dragon's eye and cause the most critical damage. Her heart pounding, she climbed, grateful for the lack of heavy armor as she was nimble and agile, racing toward the glass eye. She pulled her sword back and prepared to jab.

The eye closed, the sword pierced through, and the sparks went flying. She gripped on for her dear life as the dragon swung its head about, roaring in pain. She was going to succeed. Her bracelet still had two hits, and she had more tricks. Her thumb reached over to twist a ring on her finger to increase her strength for the next few minutes.

The air whooshed by as the dragon quickly lowered its head, tilted until her feet were touching the ground. One of its front limbs stuck out with its claws, pinching to hold the orange pot from before.

"I believe you've finally found the path of Vakfored." It chuckled and tilted its head slowly. "Go on, let go, and pull your stinger out, too."

The laughter of the beast only enraged her more. It was not trying in this fight completely. She let go of the sword and reached into her pouch but froze when the dragon clicked its tongue, a sound forcing hot air steaming over her legs.

"Take the sword out. It hurts."

The beast had admitted it hurt, but it was so calm about the pain, a sense of foreboding filled her as if a worse storm would arise if she left the sword in. She tried to push it, but the monster moved its head to counter her action, causing the sword to slice more. Letting go of the sharp edge, she snapped her wrist to prepare another shield in time as it swatted at her with its claw.

"Vakfored never listen." It mumbled. "Take the sword out, now. Then we'll talk."

Sisal still had time on her strength spell, but she was losing advantages quickly. The dragon was calmly talking to her, even after she attacked it, and she only had one more shield hit left. If the dragon wanted to talk, she could find a better advantage. She yanked the sword out. Dark red and purple glistened off her weapon, the eyelid seeping. Proof that she harmed it.

Instead of doubting her advantages further, she raised back the

sword. As it came down, the attack cracked into a tooth as the monster raised its head back up, a small grunt emitting from its mouth. Again, the dragon calmly ignored the damage.

"Good. Now clean up and you can join me in the back chamber."

It gently fixed the fallen pedestal from their fight and put the orange ceramic pot on it. Fractured lines ran around the lip. The dragon was more worried about the pot than about this fight.

She willed for another type of dust bag to come to her from her pouch. A rumble emitting from the throat of the dragon, its neck glistening brighter as a fire threatened to burst. "Unless you want to be roasted, I suggest you stop. You were victorious."

The dragon straightened the statue nearby with a sigh and then sauntered back to the cavern through an archway. "I hope you like soup, because that's all I have ready this early in the day."

Sisal paused, sword in hand, studying her target. Its eye and back were bleeding. Two severe hits landed on it, and it acted as if the injuries were nothing but mosquito bites at a picnic.

And it just invited her over for breakfast. Walking past the ceramic pot, it showed a *terra sigillata* design of a dragon and wheat around it. This place had multiple items made with the dragon's likeness on it. Rubies, jaspers, garnets, even veins of red marble carved to look like the monster. The beast was greedy and narcissistic. For years, the people of Vakfored gave tribute to the dragon named Vakandi Foreldri. It hoarded their precious materials and art and devoured those who disobeyed it. The monster only gave fear to the city. It was the same as the criminals that demanded protection in the worse districts of Vakfored.

2. THE OATH

After decades of being alone, one should be ready to host at the first sound of a gold coin falling off a pile. Vakandi should have cleaned up that mess ages ago, especially since he knew this day would come. Walking past it now was quite embarrassing. Not that the human deserved a polite greeting with what she did to him. He had one eye closed and his old back injury freshly cut open. It never healed properly and still popped from time to time during his flights. The only visible scar on his body, but there were ones on his heart. His emotions urged him to yell and blow fire... but he knew this result had to come to fruition. To calm down, he focused on the gold and what to do with it now that a visitor arrived. His friend had a fancy bag that could hold piles of the gold, and not get any bigger. If Vakandi could put all that gold away, it would really open up the place, but he still did not know if he should. Most of it was not his gold. The bank of Vakfored had not sent a representative in a long time. They were probably wondering what happened to all of their gold.

"Excuse me, little one." Vakandi glanced back, his one eye still closed. He should get an elixir soon, or else it would take a few days for the eye to heal and a week for it to function. Being stationary so long inside his cave, plus his age, made his body naturally slow down. "Is the bank of

Golden Essence doing alright?"

The lass—that was the wrong term, she was older than that—gripped her sword out in front of her.

At last, she talked. "That bank is holding strong."

"Oh... I..." Having conversations after silence for so long was nerve-wracking. "What day is it?"

"The fourth day of the Moon of Guard."

The Moon of Guard! His calendar was off by a whole moon. He really should have set an alarm spell after his last gorging of bison. "Remind me, before you leave, that I need to give you a note for the bank. And would you please put that sword away?"

The woman finally listened, pulled out a cloth and wiped her sword down before putting it away. She was about to stuff the handkerchief when Vakandi puffed out a bit of smoke.

"This is old-fashioned of me, but could you please give me that kerchief?"

A small smirk stretched across her face. "You mean the tales of using a dragon's blood to trap someone are true?"

He sighed. "In a sense, it is. But no different from how a painting freezes a moment of beauty in time."

However, even time erodes away the beauty of a moment. Silence sat between them as if his guest could sense his mood. He did not threaten her into giving the bloody cloth over. This was no proper way to host, even if the guest tried to kill him and almost broke his favorite pot. It was an original Bedruk Oresword. He walked under the archway of moonstone, which they illuminated more when he approached. A very useful light that stopped him from stubbing his toes in the dark. The smallest toe on his foot had developed to help find corners in the dark, nothing else. That pinky was never useful in a fight, just pivoting enough to hit some furniture. Like the legs of the oak table in the back chamber, which used to sit twenty people. A few of the chairs close to where he slept in the corner got stepped. To avoid stepping onto the table now, he puffed out a breath of

fire into the nearby hearth that lined the length of one wall. The blaze took instantly to the hot coals. The fire spread out along the wall.

Vakandi waved his claw and let out a small bit of magic to stir the stock pot. He was quite proud of the soup he had. Best stock around because it had been going on for a millennium. Various herbs and root vegetables have ended up in there. As well as a few fattened-up birds and a bison. From a person's point of view, the stock pot could easily fit his guest and a friend. Sure enough, her eyes stared at it, hands digging into her bag, probably preparing more of that invisible mushroom powder.

"There are some bowls on the table over there," he said. "Why don't you grab one, fill it up with the soup in the black pot over there. Sit down and relax. I know climbing my mountain is a bit taxing on humans."

The woman stayed still, hand still holding on to the bloody kerchief and her sword hilt like they were the only things that could save her. He thumped the ground with a foot. "Oh goodness. How rude of me. We haven't introduced ourselves. My name is Vakandi Foreldri, titled the Life Giver by the people of Vakfored."

The woman snorted and covered her mouth, her face flushed over her freckled face. He ignored the slight, tilting his head. "Well, will you tell me your name?"

"I am Sisal - the chosen hero to save Vakfored."

A smile cracked across his mouth, the warmth in his chest emitting out. "Excellent. You are worthy."

"Then shouldn't we be fighting instead of having breakfast?" The woman said it as she grabbed a bowl, studying the design on it. She walked near the hearth, putting a hand on it and mumbled something under her breath. Likely a prayer to the spirit of the sun. He noticed she tamped the handkerchief into her bag too, much to his annoyance.

Her head turned to the tapestries which hung on the wall, with more red and orange dragons. There used to be oil paintings too, but they did not handle the constant heat of a fire dragon's snoring. With a guest observing his home, he suddenly felt silly for having a collection of dragon images. Even if each one he treasured and marked as an important memory she should learn about. "We can fight later. You almost destroyed something precious to me earlier. That pot is almost as old as your nation. Only younger by a few weeks. Those bowls are from the third generation. While the person holding them is from the..." he recalled what the current year it was. "forty-third or fourth generation."

The calloused hands of the sword fighter suddenly acted as if they were holding onto a soap bubble that could burst if they breathed on it wrong. "How have you kept it in a pristine condition after so long?"

He swished his tail around, wrapping it under him as he curled up by the hearth. His quarters always felt cozy, but when guests arrived, he became very conscious of his size. Carefully, he pinched a small serving spoon, realizing that Sisal would never serve herself. "Are you asking because of my size?"

"No! I apologize, I just... just couldn't imagine seeing this." Her emerald eyes widened as he gently poured the soup into her bowl, over filling it instantly. People eat such small amounts, it's impossible to measure with his large forefoot.

"I am actually a delightful host. I forgot to introduce myself after you froze my back. That old injury flared up and saying 'welcome' to you was not exactly on my mind."

The woman took the dripping bowl and locked eyes with him. "You shall leave the nation of Vakfored alone!"

Her fire blazed stronger than his own. She was his end goal, of his dream that he wished would never have to come true. They would sing Sisal's name in the streets and taverns, recorded for future generations to learn, and perhaps even immortalized with a street in her honor. But for just a day, maybe one more, he could share the company of a Vakfored resident. "My wings tire and my bones ache from our scuffle. Why don't you listen to my tale? Then I shall leave."

"I don't have time for tales. And you never used your wings in our fight."

Excellent, she paid attention to details and could catch a lie. "Is there another dragon you need to go slay? Before you do, are they single? I wouldn't mind having a date."

"No. You have done plenty of tricks on the Vakfored. But no more. I will end all of that now."

Vakandi reached around Sisal and she reacted by backing up, dropping the bowl and pulling her sword out. She learned he had armed himself with a chair and slid it under her. She flopped down into it as he pushed her to the table. Calmly, he pinched another bowl and filled it up with the soup. "I fortunately have a collection of bowls. Crack that one and I am adding you to the stock."

He only meant it as a joke. She did not laugh but carefully put the bowl on the table, terrified to eat. If she truly believed he was a trickster like a fairy, well, she would probably not eat the soup. That's a shame. "I promise no harm will come to you under this roof as long as you remain peaceful."

Her hands still did not pick up the bowl. This would be an uncomfortable breakfast if she would sulk the whole time. The people of Vakfored really did not want to spend any time with him. They wanted to do other things. This specific human reminded him of the Orc Queen, who always wanted to be elsewhere when she talked to Vakandi. "I promise my tale shall end before the sunset. It will be hard to condense it all, but I shall do my best."

"I don't want to know about your stories."

"But if you don't listen, then I don't have to leave."

She glared up at him. "You swear on all the magics of the river, the land, the wind, the sun, the stars, and on life and death that you will leave Vakfored before sunset once you finish your tale?"

The magic in the air stirred up like dust, waiting for him to take flight or anchor himself to its will. To take this oath created a balance in the system of magic, granting him access to more magic and power. To break it would mean returning all his being to magic and the earth itself.

"I swear to all magics of the world that I shall leave Vakfored alone if you listen to my story."

The air sizzled as it placed a sigil in the room. Like an hourglass starting, he could only tell the entire beginning, hardly any of the middle, and the whole ending. Sisal had to know his end for her to start the new beginning for Vakfored.

2. The Oath

3. BREAKFAST

Satisfied, Sisal put her sword down on the table and reached for the soup bowl. The chair creaked from her weight shifting. The stock pot was large enough to fit her in it two times. It took a lot of soup to feed a dragon, also made it easier to drop in a whole beast in the pot - or a person. She eyed the hearth, but stayed seated to hide her jitters, and muttered a prayer of keeping herself safe again. She said the same prayer yesterday and all the days leading up to this mission, multiple times. Spirit of the sun, keep me safe; cycle of magic, life, and death, embrace me. Her sweaty handprint lingered on the hearth before it evaporated from the heat building off the fire. A small outline remained, with the dust now moved. "You promise this isn't made from people - dwarf, human, or orc?"

"Nothing of the sort!" The dragon's eyes widen in horror at the remark, more of a reaction than when she stabbed its eye earlier. "Let me find you the recipe sheet. But with two eyes. Give me one moment."

Far above where she could reach, a few barrels sat on a shelf, each painted with even more flying lizard designs. She watched the dragon pierce the lid with one claw and chug a red shimmering liquid that looked like the concentrate of a lifesaving elixir in her bag. Her potion cost her over a hundred gold. One barrel alone would be years of income for her. The dragon sighed and threw the barrel in the fire. It popped and sparkled with the new fuel.

"Now, where did I leave that paper?" With time, the injury on its back healed, the swelling diminished. He hoarded the elixir worse than Elmeagit did with her liquor at the tavern.

While she waited, she studied the soup. The smell was earthy and deep with a bone broth, a small amount of fat bubbles gathered on the surface. Daringly, she took the smallest sip of the soup. She paused, licked her lips and then chugged the whole thing. She looked over at the pot, its black metal reflecting the flames. Vakandi twisted the stand to keep the soup off from being cooked too much. The beast returned, looking for the paper. She climbed a set of stairs near the pot and grabbed the spoon designed for a dragon. It was as tall as her, making it awkward to hold and serve. She put the bowl on the table. Because of its uneven weight, it wobbled, but stopped by the time she climbed back up the stairs. Cheap bowl for such a rich dragon. At least its soup was amazing. As she poured, and accidentally over-poured, the bowl danced about.

"What magic is in this? It's the richest broth I have ever had."

"No magic. Only time. All good things are made with time."

"You are a dragon with endless time."

Vakandi chuckled. "With that logic, then I must be very good."

"Yet you live like this. Why have dull trinkets?" The beast needed its ego popped. She pointed to the broken bowl near her and then to the moonstone. "Why haven't you built a home out of something better than shale? Like use more of the rare moonstones like that and melt your gold to line the hall?"

By the corner of the cave with bird feathers, it tucked its feet under and lowered its head down. "I like how the earth feels. I draw my power from it and feel its voice. Moonstone? I cannot communicate with the stars. I hear the whimsical jokes in the wind when I fly. The fire is my kindred soul, warmth and comforting. Gold is inert to me. Also, it would be rude if I melted the gold that belonged to the Golden Essence. I'm only securing it for them. I have never lost a coin to a thief!"

"That hoard in the entrance is the legendary vault of the Golden Essence?" She barked out a laugh. "They've caught so many thieves trying to break in and steal from their vault. Each one reported it was mostly empty. Guess those thieves were telling the truth."

"Oh dear. Has that been happening? Forget about the note I wanted you to send. Do you, by chance, have a bag of endless space on you? I'll be needing some gold delivered to the bank."

A thin smile stretched across her face. "Of course. I will gladly take the gold."

With that gold, it would set her for life, along with her niece and nephew and all their friends. Her parents would live comfortably and could get off her back about doing adventuring, because she could finally focus on a craft. She sipped more soup to hide the smile. The endless hunting missions for the Guild could stop, and she could actually choose which mission she wanted. A life to sit at home and read some books. To finally have time to pick up the guitar and take music lessons, maybe even singing lessons, off in another country. The rest of the gold she had no clue what to do with. She had infinite possibilities. They pretty little coins could sit in her bag ready for whenever. They did not need any answer now.

Yet, holding that hoard of gold would make her no different from a dragon, holding on to a treasure and not using it. Even this dragon was concerned about the status of the bank and was sending the gold home. With that much wealth in her bag, it was too easy to be selfish. A dragon would not have higher morals than her.

Keeping it could ruin the Golden Essence, where almost everyone kept their gold safe. She would return the gold to the bank, every coin. Only at the cost of them telling her the truth about why they entrusted the nation of Vakfored's gold with a dragon.

The monstrous beast shifted next to her, its curled-up tail twitching. It smirked down at her, eyes glistening as if it had read her thoughts.

You will die. And if there is any corruption in the Bank, I will find it. She scowled up at him, hoping he heard that message and kept its intrusive prodding out.

"My, you must be bad at card games with all those facial expressions," it said.

"Were you reading my thoughts?"

The dragon overly exaggerated tilting its head, that it almost bumped into the wall and its snout came near her. "You're a successful hunter because you're always prepared. What did your research tell you?"

"That you're stubborn. Selfish. A traitor."

It sat up straighter. "Thorough. And nothing about telepathic abilities."

She opened her mouth to continue, but it spoke over her. "Let's start with the first story before we lose any more time. It is why there are so many ceramics here and in Vakfored."

Inclining the bowl in her hand, careful to not lose her breakfast, she studied the pottery mark to see who signed it. A pickaxe crossed with a crutch. The first symbol any School of the Arts taught. The origin of ceramics and it made a name in the art world internationally. They named multiple places in the city after him and his icon. "Is this a Bedruk Oresword bowl?"

"Yes, one of his early ones. You can see his thumbprints all over the place. It's when he used to do a coil method, too. He became such a great potter with time." More pride beamed off its face, taking credit for someone else's work.

She quickly chugged the soup and looked for the nearest tub. "Why isn't this in a museum? Why is it being used to serve soup? Where is your water?"

The dragon chuckled, pointing behind him with one foot. "Please, this is what Bedruk wanted the bowl used for, sharing meals together. Most of the food bowls are his early works. Note, his later ones are when he mastered the coloring glaze."

"Not comforting. I'm done having soup." She found the water pump and tub near where he pointed. Quickly, she grabbed the lever and pumped the water. Unlike the spoon, it was to her size. The dragon would have had an impossible time using it. "Why do you have running water?"

"For my guests to have. It was built eight hundred years ago."

Running water for its guests... not itself. Her research for this mission was completely inaccurate.

"I need a drink and not in something historical." Though in the beast's lair, that seemed to be unlikely. The soup fortunately rinsed off the bowl easily. She put her head under the water as she pumped, a cold metal taste coming to her. A whiskey would be better. Turning around, she looked at the broken bowl near the hearth caused by her reckless attitude earlier.

"Would you care for any wine? It's vintage." It inquired.

"I'm certain it's more vinegar."

"It's the perfect flavor profile for your mood."

That silenced her before a small snort emitted from her lips. She waved a hand. "Go on with your story."

4. THE CERAMIC POT

Vakandi Foreldri rather liked his simple cave. It sat on an incline on the mountain, which kept it dry in all weather and prevented bitter, chilly rain from getting in. It even had a large second cavern. He spent some time smoothing out the stalagmites on the main path to the second cavern. Winters were still cold, but with some burning trees thrown in at the entrance cavern, it would push off some of the chill. The winters were the only reason he became tempted to leave this area. Every time during a snowfall, he got tempted again, but then the sun would rise over the hills. Even if it was snow, he thought the light glistening off it was beautiful. A sign that spring would come again and soon. Today the air felt better, crisp, as if warmer days were soon to come.

He hated winter, but knew it served a purpose. Without the changing seasons, the land would not be what it was with its hills and mountains. It would be flat and boring. Magic had its own balance, even if it was bitter instead of warm. Shivering off the cold, he gently scrapped the floor to feel the earth and pulsed a bit of magic into it. He sighed out a breath of hot air. The world was less willing to take it today, but it did. During summer, it would be more willing. Stretching his wings, the frosty day making him feel stiff, the air went over and under him, ready to help lift him. The flow was faster than expected. As if a different current joined his own magical offering of earth and fire and wished to be lifted as well to a home. When he reached out with life, nothing resonated with it back. Something had joined his offering.

The magics were always slow in returning their offerings. Vakandi would wait, as he always did. He would sit comfortably here to see the sun rise. The sun sparked joy in the world. It warmed the earth; it gave the plants energy, which in turn fed the world. He adored the sun.

The beauty of the sun became interrupted as a trail of smoke rose from the Black Forest in the east. Fire in that forest would spread extremely quickly with the fauna which grew there. Taking flight, he went to help put it out, to keep peace in the valley, as well as prevent any of the death magic from emitting from the plants when they were burnt. The smell would agitate his throat and give him a painful headache for months. The forest evergreens were lush, but he could see movement near the fire. A small group of twenty people, a mix of dwarves, humans, and orcs, all wrapped up in furs to shake off the cold air.

He grumbled at seeing them and was not in the mood to deal with the foolish adventurers. He let their idiocy be the death of them instead of fighting them out for invading his land. People only want to change the land and take from it, never giving back. Their greed for land created all of their problems of war and disease. He could go hide in the comfort of his cave and wait out the fire of the forest for a few weeks.

As he turned around, he heard the deep shouts of a few men and higher ones of the women. He summoned a simple shield around him, bracing for their attacks. Bit by bit, their screams unified into a chanting word.

"Dragon! Dragon!"

Glancing back, the smoke fire puffed in and out in streams to signal him. They jumped up and down; they smiled up at him. He had seen this trap before and flew away to find the roaming bison herd for a simple meal that would be poison free. If any of the people ate from the plentiful berries, roots, and mushrooms in the Black Forest, their blood would become toxic if he ate them later. If he did, it would place him in a weaken state that even the tiny wolves could kill him. They were not like the animals of the forest who had adapted to eating and processing the noxious food. Later that evening, their fire remained small and did not burn down the forest. They waved hello to him again, and with his shield up, he dared to peek closer at the people through the evergreen and bare of leaves trees of the forest. Only one dwarf carried a pickaxe and had apparently worked hard most of the day with how there were four small overhangs for them to sleep in.

For the second time, the people did not shoot up at Vakandi. He puffed a bit of smoke and flew back to his cave. Instead of sleeping, he waited in the first chamber for the foolish adventurers to appear and attack his small hoard. He collected it from goblins and other foolish adventurers. The next day arrived with peace. The sunrise of the day again had the smoke line interrupting it. Scouting with his magic shield up, he flew over the people. No screams or shouts greeted him. Instead, only silence as a pyre construction began far from their dug alcoves. Vakandi had seen this before. Any of the orcs or dwarves who came through the forest would be sick for a day or two because of the toxins of the fauna they ate. The humans could not handle them and would die. Three of the twenty had passed.

The bodies were not on the pyres, though. In the morning, they bathed the dead in the frigid river. They remained focused on their task. Far away from the river and their home, they carried their dead and left them in small dug out holes, exposed for the crows, vultures, and wolves. For three days, the wildlife picked the bones while the people finished building the pyre. Every morning they prayed at their fire, and Vakandi confirmed it was these people who joined in on his morning offering to the magics. The small creatures unknowingly tempted him to offer some of his magic. He hesitated and decided against it, wanting to observe them more. In the evening of the third, they brought back whatever remained of the dead and put them on the pyre. For the first time since they arrived in the Black Forest, did their campfire burn out. Only the stars and moon shined down on them.

Vakandi stood near the edge of the forest, listening to find out if the rest of the group still lived. They sang and danced around, simple spells of magic illuminated near them, and they laughed in their mugs. Throughout the entire night, they celebrated. At the first peak of gray in the world, they gathered at the pyres where the remains of their dead were and waited. One human held on to a torch, staring off in the distance where the sun would rise. The moment it broke the horizon, he approached and lit the pyre. All of them chanted the names of their fallen, offering them up to the sun, stars, wind, land, and the river; to the cycle of all magic. Honoring all magics from death to life and back again.

Vakandi felt the magic open up to them, to embrace the offering. If the traveling group stayed, the magic would bless those back. Only the most ancient of beings knew of this fact. To see people doing it was unheard of. A jealous pang filled him as the burning pyre sent waves of magic out, which echoed into his own flame magic within. Their magical offering was the same as the one he felt in the mornings lately. The wave of a grander cycle of the world that only he and a few other immortals watched. Dragons were born, reigned over the land, and died after a very long time. But rarely did they die of old age, hunted by the adventurers or other beasts. His life would never be a round circle like theirs, but become a jagged point that sticks out like the shape of his scales.

The people wisely chose to not stay. They packed up to leave, unsure of what they could eat safely. The dwarf complained, pointing to the soil, talking about its deep composition. The others shook their head. To avoid being noticed and disturbing their voyage, Vakandi flew away. The smell of death was strong in the air. The wood they used to burn the bodies had been from the forest, laced with a bit of toxin, making his throat agitated as the death magic attacked his life. He was a dragon of fire and life, not death. The Black Forest made this land undesirable by the more powerful beasts who aligned with life magic instead of death. The Black Forest was vulnerable with how easily it burned too, especially with a fire dragon nearby.

Weakened by the toxins and with death in the air, the troop of people became easy picking for those who lived in the forest, such as the wolves. Their howls shook the trees and sent fear into those of weak bodies. Wolves began their typical hunting that never bothered Vakandi, and he easily ignored them.

The people could not.

Their cries interrupted the normal day to day of the life. Or maybe it was no different, since they were the prey being attacked by the wolf. The stalked prey only goes silent once the wolves ended their lives. The weak creatures would cry and alert others, to beg for help or to warn them they were also in danger. The people would be no different. They were only completing a cycle of life.

The deep rumble of the earth when the pickaxe swung down at the wolves from the dwarf drew Vakandi's attention as a yip of a dog followed it. The rest of the pack fought back and attacked his leg. The people screamed and Vakandi did not understand why they used only a small amount of fire or druidic magic. Hardly anything to actually kill the beasts. Where were the swords, the bows and arrows? An axe swung slowly at the attackers, with no accuracy.

Vakandi grumbled and wanted the magic to save them. But the magic stayed silent, not returning their blessing yet. It was naïve of him to think the magic would hasten. He had been meditating and serving it for years and knew how it behaved. Instead of listening to the magic's response, he acted on his own heart and landed near the people, toppling the trees. His skin itched in agitation from the toxins, but they did not pierce his scales. The presence of a full-grown dragon alone silenced the wolves and people. His roar was enough to cause the wolves to tuck tail and run before the true alpha predator ate them.

Only a few people whimpered. An orc holding the axe dropped it as she approached, knowing it would be foolish if she attacked the dragon. The smell of fear rolled off her, but so did an undertone of hope.

"Great dragon," she said, "thank you!"

Vakandi closed his mouth. He anticipated fear and begging. Instead, they quickly grasped that the fire dragon was their savior, which was surprising. Dragons attacked kingdoms for the gold, gems, and magical items, because they could. It was fun to show off one's strength and remind the people they were below them.

Now, no one revered him by bowing. They smiled and returned to their kind to take care of them, done with the mythical beast. The dwarf was in the worse state and asked to be carried over to the dragon.

"You have my thanks," he groaned out. "Any longer and they would have gone for my gullet."

"Where are your warriors and fighters?"

"Back in our old home, Kirrad." Answered the orc.

"And where is your new home?" Vakandi studied each of the faces. They were diverse in age and only one carried a child. To travel so far from an underground dwarven city, no wonder they were ill prepared for the land above them.

"Well." The orc glanced down at the dwarf and back up. "Guess it will be here with our current state if you welcome us."

Vakandi sighed. The innocence of these people would be the death of them. They should stay nearby where they honor the magics, and they would become blessed and plentiful, but the Black Forest was not the place for them. "Follow me. There is a valley near a river where you can begin."

He walked ahead of the people, knocking over the trees and smoothing out the path. He only itched himself a few times. The light pierced down on areas of the Black Forest for the first time in a while. The blue sky danced with clouds that called out to Vakandi to fly among them, but he practiced his patience on the people behind him. They were slower than he expected, but he forgave them as they took care of the woman with child and the injured dwarf a few times.

The orc cleared her throat. "My name is Lash of the Azure Stone clan. Guess it's just Lash now; this is my clan now. Things for us have

changed. What can we call you?"

Vakandi pondered on the request and its true meaning. These people had left their nest and could not even fly. They needed guidance before others took advantage of them. "Vakandi Foreldri."

"Thank you, Vakandi Foreldri, for everything you have done. Not sure why you are helping us. Everything I've heard about dragons is that we should be your dinner by now." She laughed. "Or is that a lie to keep people away from you?"

"We do like our privacy." He avoided admitting if dragons ate people. "But why did you shout at me earlier? Did you shout at the wolves?"

A dwarf with leaves twisted in his beard, held a staff covered with vines and runes joined the conversation. He cleared his throat, no doubt also agitated by the toxins of the forest. "When we did our morning boons, we felt something vast, like we looked into a pool and could not see the bottom. The magics rippled with you. For us, we only see our reflection." He hugged his staff tightly. "Ah! To see magic affected in such a way only meant a mythical creature lived nearby. We wanted to ask questions and learn from you!"

Lash placed a hand on her companion. "Helvin, calm down. You don't want Vakandi flying off to his private cave."

"I'm in no hurry to go somewhere." Vakandi replied. He felt a magical connection with this dwarf and the rest. He wanted to study their magical offering. Never before did small creatures offer to the magics. It was not just limited to dragons and other mythical beasts. "Maybe I should follow your lead and change. You can answer a few questions of my own in exchange for yours."

Helvin squealed and spun around on his heel. Bedruk grumbled from where he was being carried. Helvin's face became serious. "I'll be back!"

He went back to heal his friend. His healing magic needed work, and it pulled in from the death magic too much. Vakandi advised him as they continued moving

After a day of walking, the trees finally thinned out, and he pointed to the valley below, a place that could easily turn into farms. His own cave in the mountain was rich in minerals the dwarves would love to collect. They could build their homes out of the river stones and have fresh water. "Will this work?"

The dwarf ordered someone to dig a hole. Vakandi lowered his head and addressed the dwarf. "What is it you're looking for?"

"To get a sense of the mineral composition of the area. Seems like a bunch of clay out that way where there are a few trees." Finally, a core was dug out and, using a hastily made crutch, he hobbled over to look at it. With a nod, he looked at Lash. "This place will do."

The people celebrated, and Lash patted Vakandi's ankle. "Vakandi, you are our Life Giver! We will do our best to respect your land and be good neighbors."

"Yes! Name's Bedruk Oresword." the dwarf pointed to his chest. "I wouldn't mind if you help haul some river stones for us with that baffling strength of yours. Especially with how my leg is now. I can't mine or build like this!"

Lash frowned, but Bedruk and all the other people had a smile on their face. Everyone pointed to where the best place to settle would be, close to the river, but far enough they could expand. They marked where they would build the first twelve homes, forming a single ring with a very large open central area for a plaza. Lash took a hold of Bedruk's pickaxe and broke the earth. Her swing was very clumsy and messy, but she was bound to get a lot more practice soon.

After just five minutes, she already paused stretching her back. "I think the others agree with me, but would you mind offering a name for our clan?"

Of course, all creatures sought Vakandi's wise wisdom, especially in such a high importance matter. They were already looking toward him as a guardian. He wanted to give them a name from his language. Neighbors was an odd word when he could already tell they would require more than a cup of sugar regularly. They did not possess the power of a

warrior; they needed something else.

"Vakfored. I think calling you that would be very befitting with how everything is."

Only Bedruk Oresword and Helvin laughed and they kept it secret what the name meant.

"For that," Bedruk said, "I'm going to make you use those sharp claws and dig. At the rate Lash is going and chit chatting, we won't be sleeping anywhere warm and dry for months."

Vakandi grumbled and questioned his choice. Digging in the earth was not something he had done since he was a hatchling. It was something the young and people did, not a full-grown dragon. Yet, for the next week, he helped them and talked to them. Listened to their songs, and smiled as they thanked him, even when he supplied shade to for them from the sun. They danced under his wings as a way for him to join.

Each day, the people got up and praised the sun, snow, or rain, embracing the day given to them. A day used to pass by quickly, but now they slowed down and he got to see everything new and fresh through their eyes.

5. BRUNCH

Sisal stood up from her chair, paced along the hearth and offered a prayer to make sunset get here faster after hearing the dragon's first story. The very dragon she came to slay created the fire within the hearth. That had to be bad for her prayers. The creature did not continue talking. It waited to hear her opinion. The tale's quality was not even up to what she told her niece and nephew before bed. Some words to justify why they were called Vakfored, which was not the original goal of the story.

"You never mentioned a pot that entire story," she pointed out.

The lizard slurped some soup and coughed in its throat. "Goodness, if I go off topic like this, I will need more time than one day to tell the tale. With my help, they quickly built the houses, and I found out they had no plans for the plaza. It was to be a barren place, so I could always land and visit them directly in the center. Quite inviting. Those who were not on building duty were preparing the farm fields. Which again, they asked my help to haul away the heavy stones and large stumps. They did not bring any work animals with them and took advantage of me!"

She rolled her eyes. The scaly animal made it sound like a terrible thing to use your gifts to help others in need. "Focus please. What does this deal with the pot?"

The dragon harrumphed. "Anyways, Bedruk and I began running

out of work as summer arrived. I would've been content in my cave like my old days, but he sketched plans on how to make a kiln. The dwarf wanted to try out a hobby he never had the time for, but now he did." It laughed, though the sound was closer to a scoff. "Just because he had time didn't mean the others did. He asked for so much clay to be dug up. Another task I had to help with."

"If you hated it, why didn't you just say no?"

"I didn't hate it. Life had a meaning outside of magic. I wanted to live up to their title, Life Giver. During summer, they called me 'Shadow of my Sun', and I loved the honor of being named after something they embraced every day. Bedruk mocked me though, even when he had me burning fire into his kiln at all hours of the day as we experimented with clay and colors. He was determined to make a glaze like my color in the sun, and another color to mirror the blue sky. Of course, he gifted me over hundred and fifty of them to get my color right."

The dragon... it had such an ego. There had to be exaggerations or fibs in its story. The dragon had watched over the city for centuries and knew common facts about the city of Vakfored. "Of course, you knew Bedruk's name because of all the ceramics you hoard. You just grabbed Lash's name from the Hunting Guild."

"Lash could not hunt." It chuckled. "She was a woodsman and carpenter. Under Bedruk's tutelage, even a miner. Bedruk is the name of the Guild of Arts. I also know the name of your hospital, Helvin Healers. I trained him after seeing him use magic to help ease Bedruk's burden. If he was two decades younger, he would have become an Archmagus in any other city. Listen, being untrustworthy of your enemy is a good thing, but I speak the truth. I have always been a guardian of Vakfored since the beginning."

"I was told you forced the name on us, as a brand like we were your cattle."

"If you hated it, change it once we are done."

That would be the first task she would petition to the King of Vakfored. All the dragon banners, statues, mosaics, and wall paintings were to be removed in order to erase its mark on the city. The creature dragged the story out because of the loophole it created in the contract with Sisal. Vakandi could stay on the mountain if she did not listen to its story. She had to pay attention and not lose in the mind trick.

Taking advantage of the pause in conversation, she glanced around for anything within her reach to use in a fight. This room did not have any hiding spots. The table would not withstand him stepping on it. There was the random water source into the mountain. She could use it and another ice scroll to fight the dragon. That was a poor idea. The water would freeze and she would only have a small icicle that the lizard could use as a toothpick after eating her. She could use the last spell and try to destroy the elixirs to make sure it lost that advantage. It could react in that time. She still had one shield charge left.

Then what? The tricks she had in her bag required planning, not instantaneous reaction. The fight would end with the same result as earlier. She would lose. The only course of action she had was to wait and listen to the stories, to find a better opportunity.

The current long silence did not help speed up the rate the stories were told, either. Instead of grabbing more soup, she found some biscuits in her bag and chewed them.

"Once more settlers arrived, you demanded a sacrifice every moon?" Sisal asked. Only the library at the Guild of Adventurers had information about Vakandi's cave. "That's how you prevented us from going up your mountain?"

"No. We celebrated and more called me the name Shadow of the Sun, for they knew I was, and am, a servant and vessel of the sun. Each person who called me that, I would bow to them in appreciation. For they were the servants of the cycle of time that I wished to learn from."

Its golden eyes locked with her hazel. Gently, its head lowered, but never broke eye contact. She glowered and waited for the beast to continue, and it did with its defense.

"Look at this cavern." It spoke. "I have chairs and tables too small for me. I have utensils I would never use. No other dragon has a stock pot or hearth because they quickly devour their food. All of this is for when the Vakfored would come and visit."

Sisal broke eye contact, a scowl across her face. The dragon had years to plan this situation. All the cave decorations gathered as payment from Vakfored. The table and chairs meant for people and the water pump installed at the hard work of the Vakfored. It made no sense to go into this much detail to entertain the people who lived below the cave. It would be very boring to set this all up for the few random days to trick people into thinking you were a fabulous host and just end up eating them. Believing its words, though, meant her great-grandparents lied about the dragon's actions a hundred years ago. Their story passed down to her grandparents, parents, and then her. They ingrained it in her blood, like it would be for her niece and nephew.

On the ground still rested the shards of the other original Bedruk bowl she destroyed. Without knowing its history, she casually destroyed it to agitate Vakandi. It swore to keep her safe and could not lash out. She wanted to see how far she could push the dragon like it did to the people of Vakfored. Instead, her actions disrespected her own heritage. She found a clean handkerchief in her bag and collected all the pieces of the bowl. The small shard pieces were the hardest to pick up, but bit by bit they stuck to her finger and placed into the cloth to be put down on the table. Magic of fire, water, and earth she put into the broken shards, with a splash of time from her own lifeline. The pieces flew together as the time reverted around the pot. It shook and rattled and clunked together as the potter's mark of a pickaxe and crutch appeared. The swirls of orange and brown gathered around the twists of red. It snapped together at last. Tiny holes were on its side, guaranteeing its life as a soup bowl had ended, but it could now sit by its cousin out in the front cavern.

"Thank you for that offering and for doing that." Vakandi said.

Once Vakandi was gone, she would take their history back. Everything in the cave had to be inspected for any kind of mark or signature. A collection of wooden frames hung along the opposite wall, with the ugliest art she had ever seen, but fairly represented Vakandi's style. The oil had melted and dripped on the shale floor, burnt brown with tints of red on it pooled below each one while the canvas was stained yellow. The lack of varnish to protect it from Vakandi's breath ruined it, but a blatant sign of the dragon was full of hot air and she should not trust everything it said.

It watched her walk near the destroyed art of Vakfored. "I really should have asked them to put the paintings else where once the first one melted. But they wanted me to look at them, bring some color to my sleeping quarters. I think after a bit, they realized what was happening."

There were more tapestries than painting puddles. Of course, they were not completely pristine either, with a few burnt spots and frayed ends. They added color to the cave, something beyond the orange, brown, and gold. Again, each had the flying lizard on it, this dragon hoarded dragon artwork. One by the entrance of this cavern had a tight weave mixed with dark red colors with tidbits of orange and gold. It displayed an image of a young Vakfored city and its five rings sitting below Vakandi's outstretched wings, casting a shadow over the city. A similar image to the outline of Vakfored's banner. Predator preparing to pounce on its prey.

Next to the hearth, draped a cloth as long as her, looked more like a dirty curtain with how it did not have dowel rod intertwined in the bottom. The weaved fabric might have been white before all the ash and stained orange, black, and purple splashes ruined it. Gingerly, she grabbed at the loose threads that hung near the fire. "Is this a dish towel?"

A claw pinched at an edge of the large fabric. She ducked out of its way as it carried the fabric to be near the table. The dragon breathed hot air on it. Quickly she pinched her nose, not wanting to smell more sulfur. She had enough of it when she first arrived. As he continued to blow air, a silver thread hidden within the cloth wrapped around the spots and illuminated symbols to create a swirl on the fabric. She let out a whistle.

"A magical rag! Does it get the heavy burnt stains off your soup pot?"

"It's an old language, from the Age of Ballads. When you put the fabric over a hearth to warm it, it will display the song of welcoming you home and what awaits you every day."

"This is a song? What is the tune? What instrument did they play?" She reached a hand out and looked over the symbols. Nothing looked familiar. There were so many symbols too. It must have been closer to a ballad. "I don't recognize the language."

"Very few elves know it, even fewer wizards. It's a song that reminds us to avoid repeating history, but to embrace the cycle of life. To accept the darkest nights as much as the sunniest day."

"Avoid repeating, but let the cycle repeat? That makes no sense."

"It's why we study the past, to strive for a better future. The Vakfored created this song after teaching me how to embrace death magic. All knowledge is power."

6. THE WOVEN RAGS

The Black Forest had thinned on the eastern side of the town. Other immigrants had arrived and settled. They made more long homes, creating multiple circles growing outward from the center. A place where they would gather to praise the sun and the moon, and even Vakandi Foreldri. They never paved or smoothed the center path. They had not fully figured out how to make a platform strong enough to support a dragon's weight. Seeing the city from up high was a beauty, almost like the inside of a tree or onion with multiple layers. The style of each ring is unique to its own. Thatched roofs, split levels, towers, window layout, clay shingles, metal peaked roofs, and gardens. The differences continued and made it easy to know what era the building was from. In the west sat the tallest tower of the entire city. Not a watchtower made of stone, but a mage's tower fed with the magic stream of the earth where their research progressed. In the mornings and at the full moon, the faithful mages sung from thc top of the tower welcomed the day.

Vakandi Foreldri recently slowed his visits to the Vakfored once his initial friends had passed. He missed Helvin, Bedruk, and Lash. It had been the first time he had made friends with short-lived creatures. It made the months feel too short and days even shorter. Each time one died, he showed up for the night vigil and burning. The pain in his heart forced him to leave to meditate on this loss. It also tucked his tail and caused him to cower. He loved the people and watching them grow up and discover new things. They shared finger paintings and cheap pottery, but Vakandi loved it. Now, seeing it and knowing the person would vanish before they learned everything about the world, it hurt. For him to befriend another long living creature like him meant to invade their territory. The place where dragons meet would be where the cities rested, the neutral grounds. Dragons considered the cities an infestation, no different from a colony of ants settling into a person's home.

He didn't see the people as an infestation anymore, but as symbols of the cycle of the world. The sun rests, the night begins, the sun rises, the day is there. The sun is a circle, the lives of each person are too, and both leave rippling effects of what they did on those around them. Because of Bedruk, brilliant azure and vermilion ceramics excelled in the southwest of the city. The potters and bakers bickered over the kilns and ovens. Other countries desired these masterful works and used the Paondel River to arrive and pass through the city. Bedruk's legacy lived on, but his work orders and conversations were gone. It was a time where Vakandi's heavy heart sat at the low point of the circle. He avoided the growing town, but kept up with his patrols of the mountains, the Black Forest, and the bog, making the beasts and monsters stay away from Vakfored. He questioned the balance of the world for a few decades, his thoughts interrupted by a few visitors from the mining guild. Finally, he decided it was time to meet the town again.

Five rings and a water wheel made up the town, at least a couple hundred people from the original seventeen, plus many immigrants who were becoming Vakfored. He had never planned to make friends with the first batch, only to be their mentor in magic. But then they taught him about other gifts of earth and wind through art and songs. Maybe he could try to be a friend again. The cave always felt cozy before he got to know the people, but now it was empty, and he desired connecting with them again.

He landed in the inner ring to meet with the leaders. Even though it was mid-morning, the town launched multiple lights into the air to create a serpent weaving around. The magic display created a shadow over the town as the imaginary beast flew. They played the drums loud enough to shake Vakandi's scales. Tables were being pulled out as he settled into the central area and looked around, waiting for someone to greet him personally. Children roared up at him, taunting him to do the same. He patted his feet, tapped his tail, lifted his head and let out a great roar filled with fire up into the air. The magical serpent crashed into the flames and dispersed with the disruption of magic.

The town cheered, a few kids ran away scared, but their parents' presence quickly comforted them. He lowered his head to speak to the town's chief leaders as they approached. A few came prepared in their vestibules, others fumbled to put them on to distinguish themselves as a leader of a Guild Hall. Hands grabbed at his feet, causing him to shudder. Quickly, he turned to see a few older children and people placing their hands on him. Even one mage pulsed magic to him. It was a trickle compared to Helvin, but he sent a bit of the wind magic back to them.

"Oh, Shadow of our Sun! It is wonderful to see you here. We have much to tell. You probably saw it while flying, but we have a water wheel." Shouted an older woman.

"Along the river, yes. But tell me about it." What he really wanted was to hear their passion for their accomplishment. The water wheel worked with a purifier to deliver fresh water to all the houses. The miners, dwarf, human, and orc alike made it easy to add new houses to the line.

The woman beamed upon being recognized. "We can even add a pipeline to your home."

"I would like that." He had no issues drinking water from the river, but it would be nice to have something of theirs in his home. Something else to look at besides Bedruk's pottery. The woman talked about how easy it would be to add. Currently, the miners were digging out at the base of the mountains in the northwest. It would take a little longer to add the water line from there.

The guild master of the woodmen, determined by the embroidery axe and tree sewn on his vestibule, spoke up. "Ah, we should do an illusion of our looms for you! We have a production increasing to keep up with wool and hemp cloth demands of our growing town. Quickly, gather some fabric for the Life Giver."

Vakandi shook his head. "I appreciate the offer, but your people need it more. A dragon does not wear cloth either."

The people laughed and patted his scales, complementing him on his warmth on this late spring day. The warmth in his stomach grew at their touch. It was the gentle touch he appreciated that came from Lash and Bedruk, not the sharp weapons or bitter cold magic he used to face. To be humanized and welcomed even after being gone so long felt unifying. The Vakfored were friends who were always there, no matter what.

A child squealed and ran back to their parents, a smile on the older orc's face. The dragon watched as the orc patted the head of their little one. Hands so small, able to grasp their child carefully and lovingly. Vakandi had claws able to dig graves.

"Shadow of our Sun," the guild master of mining, a half dwarf and human with a book in one arm and two pickaxes on his vestibule, approached. She tilted her head backward to look up to him. "I'm glad to see you again in my lifetime. My grandfather talked of the deeds you have given us."

"Has it been that long since I was last here?" The woman had no gray in her hair and a thin beard, but was a fully grown adult with lines around her face. She looked younger than Bedruk when Vakandi first met him.

"Aye. But like the sun, each day you arrive is a blessing."

"The magical serpent was beautiful," he complimented. "Is there a

festival coming? I apologize for destroying it. I didn't realize it would go that way."

She waved her hand to dismiss the apology. "Aye. One of celebration. Our mages and apothecaries have made an incredible discovery. Instead of wasting food and having it rot from the high heat or winter, we can now preserve it with magic to keep it fresh longer."

As a dragon who only eats raw meat, this was an interesting concept and problem to have. Venison was easy to capture nearby or fly to the mountains and grab some goats climbing around like jumping beans on the white cliffs. The people hunted in the southeastern forest and the plains in the south where the bison roamed, but they needed a diverse diet besides meat. Their farms stretched on both sides of the river in the south.

"Oh, that's innovative. How is its flow to magic?" He asked.

The mage guild head master, a human old enough to be seeing some grandchildren, approached with her silver and gold puff balls on her vestibule. It sparkled with magic as she stepped forward into Vakandi Foreldri's shadow and knelt down on the ground to the dragon. "Shadow of our Sun, this morning shines bright with your presence. I, Engill, have sworn to keep the lessons you gifted Helvin going. Keeping in mind about the balance of magic and life. We have applied these regenerative arts on our food and even on the gravely hurt to create a better recovery."

The Vakfored, always creating. These ideas were like pebbles tossed in a pond, creating ripples in the water growing out and creating waves. "This is wonderful. Tell me, how did you create it? Do you have food to sample?"

Engill leapt up and clapped. "Food! I'll be back quickly. We've produce from the fall."

She ran off with excitement. The others were bouncing with similar energy and scattered about to gather instruments to play music. The style had changed with the more addition of metal instruments. Beautiful music with a rhythm that started again on the fourth beat. Vakandi bobbed his head to the rhythm, wings extended and others came to dance under him. A few children sung. The vibe of the Vakfored had him excited to try vegetables. It was impressive to keep a season-old food still fresh. The new crops were growing out in the distance, their small saplings pushing through the soft soil. The recent snow was melting, the warm summer was coming on too fast. Dark stripes were lining the mountain in places and the river overflowed in the foothills. A bump in the magic stream disturbed his thoughts, a hiccup in the balance the town had. A young human approaching the age of adulthood hobbled up to one of his claws. "Is it alright if I touch you?"

"Of course. Thank you for asking."

"The blood amber color is gorgeous on your claws," she said. "A dark red that reflects the light."

Proudly, he flexed his claws a little more and could not help but chuckle at the praise. "Well, that's because I -"

Her hand touched his claw. It felt as if he hugged a prickly plant, as the magic that was within her sparked up to his mind. Instinctively, he flew up in the air suddenly to escape the magic that countered his very being. The girl's cry mingled with the others who stood beneath his wings. The sudden movement and shifts of cool air lashed down at them. Quickly, Vakandi flew higher to avoid harming the people. The mage leader returned, her hands reaching up to him. The farmers were behind her, wearing their green and red clothing. "Please, we have brought what you asked!"

What they brought did not matter. There was an infection in the town and this child carried it.

"This human," he hissed, "tell me what has happened. Death magic courses through her."

7. THE RIVER

Engill's voice cut above the bickering of others, her face set and determined to be heard. "She fell from her boat in the fast currents of the Paondel River. The sharp rocks in the current stabbed her leg. We rubbed her wounds with our new healing herbs grown with death magic and nutrients from the Black Forest to stop her from bleeding out and losing her leg."

Up in the air, Vakandi wanted to burn the leg off now, to remove the darkness that had already crept into the city. The pumpkins, apples, and potatoes were still being set out near the edge of the inner circle, along with a table covered with fresh meat for him. Only the meat felt clean. Death magic touched the rest. The fire in him grew as he prepared to destroy it.

The guild masters of the woodsmen and miners hopped on the table, shortly followed by the farmers. All their arms raised up, begging. "Don't! Please stop!"

They were foolish to think using death magic could prolong life. Death was the opposite side of the coin from life. The city was no different from any other city infestation on a dragon's land. They became greedy for what was not theirs. It would be a matter of time until they desired the long life Vakandi had. They ignored all of his lessons on life magic, the people did not listen. He taught them the healing arts and how things should end as deemed by the world. Rage boiled as he thought more, recalling the history they were bound to repeat.

The people of Vakfored only arrived at that thought because he had not taught this current generation, or the one before. He had abandoned them for the time being and left them to explore. The Black Forest was full of death magic-based fauna. It was readily available for them, unlike their Life Giver. He only prowled their land to keep them safe, but did not talk to them. With how angry he was, ready to blow fire and harm his Vakfored, he flew closer to the snowy mountains, focusing on his wings beating up and down, redirecting his fury there. He did not want to think that this town was a mistake. That he could have done more exploring of his land and the world if the people did not depend on him. Anger drove those thoughts.

A spell of noise amplification reached his ears, a begging, whimpering message from Engill. "I know you've lived longer than us and maybe you know of the world better. Listen to us. Please listen!"

The beseeching cry of Engill was as soft as a mouse next to the rumbling of the mountains. The earth shook, but not because of magic or a powerful spirit, but because of Vakandi's rage. White clouds billowed out and quickly down the mountain, racing toward Vakfored.

An avalanche.

The gentle curving Paondel River acted as a guide for the snow to roll down. Even after all these generations, they never built canals or a dam along the foothills from the mountain to the city. The entrance to his cave vanished within a second as the snow built up more speed.

"Dam!" Vakandi Foreldri shouted. His emotions earlier blinded him from his actions.

He wrapped his wings around himself and dove toward one foothill near the town to stop the stampeding water, ice, and snow. The white caps of the splashing waves grew, threatening to destroy everything the

Vakfored had built. Water and ice were Vakandi's weakness. He was a dragon of fire, earth, and life. He had no magical control over water, but he had to physically stop it. His claws dug into the earth around the river, just north of the smallest hut of the town, an outpost for the miners. There were lives beneath him, there were more behind him in the town. He could not shake the ground to divert the river and avalanche without destroying the ones beneath the ground. Pulling the terrain from the town directly behind him would destroy Vakfored. They did not deserve this death. The people were naïve in the magic and were discovering the world on their own. Just as he had when he was born.

Turning around, tail tucked under to protect it, wings stretched out, he became the shield for Vakfored. For his children.

The force of the water prickled his scales and magic like the death magic did earlier. Each chunk of ice that hammered into him, piercing his being. Carefully, he willed the small rocks on the surface closer to him. With the heat of his soul added to the rock, it became molten and creeped up his claws, his feet, and his legs.

A sharp pain slammed into him in his lower back as the dominant force of the avalanche arrived. A roar escaped his mouth as he burned and spat back at the ice that assaulted him. His balance slipped with the impact and he staggered forward with one step. His lava stretched out to his wings, but he had to pull it to his lower back to create a better defense, where the most pain emitted. The pain no longer prickled, instead it felt as if multiple spears stabbed him. His energy drained to keep up the defense against ice and water.

Multiple small creatures ran toward him. Their bold colored clothing stood out in the buildings, trees, and snow. Those mounted on horses arrived at him first just as the strength of the avalanche slowed.

"Shadow of our Sun!" Voices cried.

His lava eased back as they approached to avoid hurting them. The touch of healing magic fed into him immediately, the very arts he had taught Helvin. The guild master for the miners climbed up the dragon's closest leg that lacked lava, as if Vakandi was a ladder not a scaly beast. She tossed a rope down and shouted, "He bleeds!"

Vakandi looked back. The area was a mix of black lava and thick reddish-purple ice.

Engill stopped healing and immediately climbed up the rope. Others followed suit. Compared to their hands, their feet were not as gentle, and some slipped and yanked on his scales. He did not complain, but grimaced. The pain from that was nothing to the throbbing and piercing sensation on his back.

"Dig around. I need to see the wound." Engill spoke.

The avalanche had stopped, and Vakandi could only hear occasional cracking sounds of trees or ice breaking. He caused it, and none of this would have happened if he had kept a watchful eye on the town instead of selfishly sulking for decades. There were people who depended on him. Time did not stop because he thought it did.

They swung pickaxes at full force near Vakandi's scales to break through the ice and the cooled lava rock. Others did not want to leave Vakandi's side and brought out a giant white canvas, brushes and paint. With the foot he used to adjust his balance earlier, they painted it the Black Forest and clouds, images of the city. It tickled to have their brushes go near his feet, distracting him from the work on his back. The Vakfored applied fire magic as they got closer to the scales near his back.

"Shadow of our Sun... a plate has snapped off!" Engill declared. "We will find it and repair it."

He tried to swish his tail around, but the massive amount of snow and earth trapped it and whatever else was the avalanche brought down. His lava shield melted the ice, packing it hard into a shape around him. He could not move, his wings stuck outward.

Throughout the day and late into the evening, they raised and moved away thick chunks of ice with magic. People came out of the mines and

worked to free Vakandi while all the healers used their magic. The lessons that Vakandi gave to Helvin echoed back at him. He learned new lessons of art as the children giggled and taught him how to paint with a branch as if it was a paintbrush on the canvas. His strokes were sloppy, but they praised his white blotches of clouds. It was supposed to be the moon, but he did not correct them.

"Still no sign of your plate," Engill stated, sweat dripping down her forehead as she exerted herself to repair his scales. "We'll keep looking. For now, we are getting the death slowing herbs on your back."

"No!" He hissed, flames dancing out between his teeth, the brush turning to a torch and ash. A quick reminder of how he had to keep his temper in check. He would not let his short patience and pain cause him to lash out on the Vakfored. Still, the children sensed it and backed up, scared at the sudden anger. "Do not touch me with that magic."

"If we don't line your body with the herbs, it could seal up and reject the plate by the time we repair the plate."

"My body rejects death magic already. I am like the sun, a bright and fiery life. Not of darkness and icy death."

Engill and the others stopped applying healing magic, glancing at each other and then lowering their heads. "Forgive us, for we did not know. We won't stop until we find it. Maybe we are wrong about how damaged your plate is."

Engill waved for the children to return, confirming they were safe. A few adults stayed nearby to give them more confidence. The children did not ask for another brush for him. They went with the safer option of telling stories or singing songs to entertain him.

With a combination of fire, magic, and careful placing of pickaxes, they continued to look for the plate nearby. They built an enormous bonfire near him to keep him warm. He had not realized how much his joints hurt until he felt the warmth tickle to them. With a trail of guilt, he said. "I did not think of my actions. I am so sorry for causing this avalanche."

Multiple voices spoke up, hands patted on his scales. There were two common phrases:

"You're forgiven."

"We'll always love you."

Those words warmed him the most. By the middle of the night, he could move his wings, but he had lost his plate. The open wound hurt too much to fly back to his cave. He stayed on the outside of the city, receiving constant treatment from the healers, but the wound was too deep and became a permanent scar without the plate. A reminder of how he lost control of his anger and lashed out at the ones he loved.

Morning arrived, and the city paused its search to do their daily offerings to the magics. Unexpectedly, the daylight cracked through the clouds and highlighted the location of the plate. Cracks ran along the plate. Without the aid of the death herbs, they were not sure how to re-attach it if they could repair it. Vakandi had no answer, either. "In case anything bad happens when I am not looking," he said, "or if you want me to come visit, keep that in a place where you can reach it. If you apply fire to it, touch it, and talk, I will listen and I can come."

Engill gently touched the scale. "I can't wait to theorize with you about some other magics, then."

"I would enjoy that. I think I have a few lessons to learn from you as well." With his tail free from the ice, he wrapped it around himself, embarrassed by his actions of earlier. "Thank you, Vakfored, even after I ruined your special day."

Engill patted his foot. "That avalanche would've happened. We were planning on creating a new vent hole in the mountain soon. We want to expand the city below with the emptied mines."

"And you hadn't built a dam yet?"

"Never had an avalanche."

"The mountains are right there. The river could overflow to ruin your crops. You need to learn to redirect nature's force."

"Like we did with the plants and the young woman's leg?"

Vakandi never appreciated back talking, especially from the people when it proved him wrong. "Yes. I shall show you plans for a dam once I have healed. But I suggest you direct your resources here immediately so your city may thrive more in the future."

8. THE VAKFORED

The historical fabric laid across Sisal's lap near the fire. The silver characters faded to blue as the cloth cooled. Now that she knew what the symbols were, it made it easier to spot certain characters. Her fingers traced over a velvet stitched character, hoping magic would burst out and she could hear its tune. Would it be a moderato and be quick or have a lento pace? It might even combine the two with how it displayed the lyrics. If only she knew more than terminology about music, but the actual theory. She lowered the woven song, keeping it near the fire to see its characters. The hearth had warmed her own cheeks with how close she sat. At the bottom of the largest circle sat the deep purple curve she accused of being a stain, three characters stretched over it. "I should've recognized it. This is on the Engill's Perigon sign. I always associated it as an icon for death."

"I'm pleased to know that place is still in service." Vakandi sighed with relief. His head rested next to thc table, within arm's reach of her and her sword. He had gifted her some history of Vakfored, and she pondered ending him.

"We have funerals. People still die. Your fear of us extending our lives to be as long as yours never came to be. A terrible assumption."

He was so close she could attack his eye again, but it would not work, it would be pointless. Within his reach on the tall shelf sat the elixir potions. She needed to fight him, not in this room. She had to bait him into the gold cavern. He could do it himself, talking about all the historical items he had. There had to be more out there besides gold and exceedingly valuable Bedrock pots. Once there, she could use her staff to fly and continue her original plan, all when he was not looking. It would not be simple, since he had yet to leave her side. At least the last story was decent.

"What about dragons, though? What is your life cycle? Your end?"

A small pule of smoke trickled from his nostril. "It's you. As long as you finish listening to my story."

His words did not seem sad. In fact, he sounded smug, his mouth pulled back into a smile, revealing the sharp curved teeth and a glimpse of his pink gums. It looked as if he showed off that he learned about embracing death from Engill. During the story, Vakandi read out the song, but did not sing it, saying his voice would not work in that way. The song of life and death stitched into cloth for eternity, made from the same magic that Engill created. There already sat a lesson in reading the lyrics.

Only a life with a passionate heat could make the words appear. There is no life without passion, without a spark of hope for another time, with a kindling of acceptance of death comes with life. For everyday is unique, every day is a joy. Embrace what's been gifted and sing the song.

Mirroring the dark purple spot for death, on the opposite side of the circle sat a brilliant orange surrounded by yellow. The characters in the center of the yellow were pronounced as *lifandi,* translating to the word 'living'. She wanted to ponder and debate what it all meant. Asking any sort of questions would delay Vakandi from telling his story, finding the loophole in the magical agreement. She had to listen to the entire story. Anyone more educated than her would know the best question, possibly even a second one, to get the truth of Vakandi's music and history. Fingers tightened on the edge of the smooth and heavy fabric. She risked a single question that she could take the answer back to Vakfored and help them study the tapestry more.

"Can you at least tell me the song's meaning?"

"Life is not always the beginning for someone as much as death is not an end. "Vakandi's death would be the beginning of Vakfored's freedom. An opportunity to do more and no longer heed to his demands and live in fear of his presence up on this mountain. They could take down that gaudy sign lighting up the mountain. If he had been willing, he could have written more of their music. Saved the choreographed steps of the dances, the designs of any instruments that originated from Vakfored. Instead, he hoarded other items, ones she originally thought narcissistic, but proved to be gifts, not sacrifices. Items he held close to his heart, even the original made pottery pieces. A dragon of his size could not write all the music sheets or perform a dance like the Vakfored did. They were not things he physically could hold on to. They vanished when the music ended. He could not give her the answers she wanted.

The characters for Engill's Perigon became a bare after-image as the cloth cooled down. That place was a common philosophy of the Vakfored, but according to merchants and bards, was unheard of elsewhere.

"They say Engill's Perigon and the Golden Essence have a deep and old relationship. It's said that anyone who goes there will never pay for a funeral. Everything covered from the food and drinks to the pyre building. There are no private burnings, for death is never lonely. Were you the one who sent the gold there? Was it the bank's gold?"

"Originally, yes, it was my gold. I haven't been to a burning at sunrise in a very long time, or sent funds. Others must have continued the tradition. Whoever they are, they have my eternal gratitude. I would like if they received this," he nudged the fabric, the last of the characters looking like stars vanishing in the sun. "Please let them know how to apply the heat."

She gripped it tighter, pulling it from him. He was giving away a heritage piece, which he held onto for centuries. That meant something to him. A sign he would leave his cave at least, and not immediately burn the Vakfored for sending Sisal to kill him. "I promise."

Sisal placed the fabric on the table and folded it up small enough to put into the opening of her bag. Initially, the bag bulged, but then the rest of the fabric slid into the bag and vanished. She made sure the bag sat secured next to her, more worried about it now than she ever was when her life savings sat in it. She went over to the hearth to say a thanks for finding such a valuable piece of their history, a song no less. It was the first she ever heard of one for Vakfored. The words of thanks hardly finished forming as she paused, looking toward Vakandi. "There's a saying in every household that with a bit of oil, a prayer to the hearth is a prayer to the sun. They called you 'Shadow of our Sun', are you taking credit for our traditions?"

"Credit, or being the origin? I am outside of the Vakfored timeline." He sat up straight and carved out a circle on the table, and did an oblong shape with a small peak outside the circle, with multiple points overlapped. It was the same shape as his scale. "We cross paths at various peak moments, but their perfect circle of seasons continues on."

"According to you, we would have died without you."

"And I wouldn't have lived without Vakfored."

"Why didn't you use one of your many elixirs to heal your back and plate?"

He sighed, as if annoyed at her for pointing out the obvious. "The Vakfored had not figured out how to make the elixir yet. Because of our conversation after the avalanche, they redirected their research to life magic herbs. They traded a decent amount to get them. I have not talked this much in a long time and need a bit of rest before preparing lunch. Then I will talk off your ears with another story."

She resisted laughing at his acknowledgement. His last story was better than the first. It made him relatable. Reminding her of when she had short patience for the trouble her niece and nephew would cause. She would not have brought an avalanche down on them, but her dumb anger almost broke her brother's vase.

The walls of this cavern still had a few tapestries hanging on it, including the one with his wings outstretched over the city. There was a possibility that the image was not of a dragon readying to devour the Vakfored, but shielding the city from the harshness of the world. The banners of Vakfored were a symbol of being a shield. She actually wished she had more time to ask more questions, that maybe a day would not be enough.

"What does Vakfored mean in the old tongue?"

Vakandi paused beneath the elixirs, the fire's light glistening off his dark red scales. Before she would have thought threatening, now she saw a tired dragon. His eyes wandered over to the woven tapestry of him looking down over the city. "It means you are my hatchlings. My children."

9. THE MIRROR

Sisal stood at the entrance of the first cavern, observing everything that made Vakfored. The sky was various shades of sapphires with the brilliant sunlight and dotted with clouds. The sun's rays reflected off the golden dome roof of the Golden Essence. Out by the Black Forest, near the eastern edge, the ever-flame glowed. The magic pulsed off it, a combination of powers piercing away the evils of the world, no matter if they lived in the light or dark. Engill's Perigon sat on that side of the city, where the ceremonies of the dead took place in the large public park next to the forest. The ceremony would finish in the morning when they burned the bodies to say goodbye and celebrate the new world that would begin. Local inns and pubs were nearby for family and friends to gather, talk, and laugh. Come night, only silence and darkness filled the park as the Paondel River flowed to accept the spirit of those who passed to their next world. A tradition that existed beyond the founding of Vakfored.

Sisal's parents taught her to pray to the hearth. To share the good and bad news with the spirit of the sun. They did not know the true origin of the tradition. The spinal plate of Vakandi rested in the Palace of the King, where they would report to Vakandi without even knowing they were. For a century he listened in, when he should have acted. The last act the dragon guardian did on the city was to burn it. The Vakfored tried to expand beyond the mountains and the forest. However, the onslaught caused them to build their very own bird cage, restraining their growth. A wall around the city to save them from the dragon. They were a pet sitting in that cage, looking out at the mountain dreaming they could be free, but afraid they would get burned if they left.

This caged bird was ready to strike if the beast came near. The King worked with her and the city to prepare for this day. They knew today she would arrive at the cave in the mountain. They crafted a back-up plan for if she failed. Weapons lined the defensive wall of Vakfored. A few mirror spells were ready in places too. Even a few houses were purposely abandoned and set with flying traps to hurt Vakandi if he breathed fire on them. The inner ring was the most dangerous place. Enough magic to pin Vakandi down and silence him. Trapping the beast within the very cage it forced the Vakfored to make. Hopefully, it would not come to that.

There were still places left helpless. The peaceful pier on the river allowed boats to arrive from other cities. They carved a path through the Black Forest with various outposts to further expand trading routes and visitors. It's how they learned that other cities and countries had a history of weapons and defense. Vakfored only had pickaxes, hoes, and shovels. It forced them to remain small and figure out ways to grow more food in the small valley for the ever-growing city. Without Engill's research, the city would be half the size it was today.

Sisals' eyes wandered over to the land in the south where the farms sat along with irrigation patties, fruit trees, hemp, and bamboo. The blocked-out city made it an easy target to snipe and destroy. Along with learning the constellations and history, they learned to find the mountain on which the dragon sat, ready to harm them if the Vakfored acted out. Like a dog tied to a post, alone, and waiting for their master.

When Sisal was young, she lived in the innocence of never knowing how bad things truly were until she became a young adult. Then she learned of the rigid rules that kept everyone in place. They forbade anyone from going to the mountain and cave. Music was shameful, no theater or orchestra. In the southwest, the bison were to be left alone for Vakandi to eat. The walls they built around themselves to keep them safe from the beasts of the Black Forest and the monsters that lived in the swamps and mountains. The enchanted stone was sturdy enough to withstand dragon fire and defeat local creatures and thieves. They regularly updated the stone with new magical technology and research in case of future invasions. To prevent a new deep black line like Burnt Road from happening again. A black crescent, a constant reminder of what happened to her great-grandparents' generation, split a third of the city. The King of the time desperately focused all efforts on building the wall and defense, with the help of both the Guild of Arts and Guild of Adventures.

Since becoming an adult, Sisal felt as if the city was constantly walking a tightrope. A Vakfored being a city that only created art and celebrated, seemed another world away, if it was not for the art that remained. The walls had motifs, mosaics, graffiti, and murals with faded and flaking away paint. In school, her teacher made them all help paint over one to repair it. The songs in the taverns were not their own, but songs of heroes abroad. Only the music done at the Engill's Perigon belonged to the Vakfored. There were statues of the greats, but most of them were of the dragon Vakandi. She once shoulder checked a statue of Vakandi to become a soldier of the Vakfored army. She tried repeatedly to knock it over. No one had succeeded, no one was as stubborn as her. With a bit of magic, she infused a dynamite material from the mines into the stomach of the dragon. The explosion caused the stone to damage the barracks walls and some nearby houses, but the city cheered her success. Her captain still made her do dish duty and run laps every day.

She won't be doing dishes much longer. She will soon have a feast with clean dishes, and the people of the city will chant her name in the streets. Maybe the mages can perform a light magic show like they used to do centuries ago to celebrate the tyrannical dragon being gone.

Vakandi Foreldri's slow steps approached her. "Excuse me, Sisal," the dragon's voice came to her. It was a soft whisper as if to not startle her, but it still surprised to hear him say her name finally. Though his step was nothing silent or gentle. "If you would like, there is a door built only accessed by people of your size. A safe refuge for you to sleep."

"Safe by your definition?"

"Safe by the dwarves, orcs, elves, and humans of old definition. Around the Age of Ballads, they requested if they could build a safe port for all of those who visited me. A spell is in there to connect to the King or Golden Essence in case. I cannot open the door. I cannot use magic to break it."

That was the door she saw when she first entered his cave. She should have gone in there during their initial fight, she might have had better odds.

"Could you still bring the mountain down to crush and stop me?"

He chuckled as he pointed at a door the size of his claw. "It would destroy the entire plan."

"What plan?"

"Rest. It's not worth bringing the mountain down and destroying my treasures with you in it."

She stayed where she was, silent as she stared out at the defenseless city. He could easily blow fire down on them. Fire shield spells did not protect everyone. He could land his giant form and smash everything about. They were insects to him. He could demand tribute easily.

But he never did. The royal hunting grounds where the bison roamed were not for the King and Queen, but for Vakandi. In her entire life, she never actually saw him do anything good or bad. All she ever heard were stories from her grandparents. All she heard now were stories from the dragon itself, and she needed to decide which stories were true.

Why did he turn his back on the city? He represented the ultimate power and could destroy the Black Forest and save them from all the trouble it brought. He could completely remove all the monsters in the swamp and mountains. Instead, he let them roam freely and harmed the

great people of Vakfored. He forced them to use their shorter lifespans and limited resources to build the walls. Recalling everything the beast forced upon them reminded her to not give in to the monster's honeyed words. "What will you be doing if I rest?"

"What a dragon normally does. Meditate and connect to the ley streams of magic."

"Why?"

"Why does anyone study the world? To discover and learn more. To grow."

"Did you become weak or forgotten how to defend us?"

"No. I have the power to bring down the mountain." He threatened.

Her jaw clamped shut. Talking was a waste. He was not strong; he was distracting her from her truth. She walked over to where he pointed and found the handle for the door. Intense magic flooded her mind. Magically drilled into the walls around the door were cages, roots, anchors, knots, and every way to tie and force a grounding. Sharp edges of ice and death magic pierced out of the room, ready to launch out. The door creaked on its hinges.

The dragon spoke behind her. "I couldn't clean it. I can't go in there."

Multiple beds lined the wall, with two tables in the middle, similar arrangement as the barracks. The room was proof that it could welcome more than one soul into the cave. For example, the giant rats' nest in one bed had at least six bodies. Spider webs gathered in many areas. They were long enough to create a ladder from a bed to a table. As she entered, eight legs skittered toward her. She stepped out of the way and grabbed at her sword. The blade shimmered a slight glow as a creature that only belonged in the Black Forest charged at her. The monster was as large as a hunting dog.

"Kónguló!" The name echoed through the hall as Vakandi cried. His voice cracked. "Get out of the way so I may burn it."

That quickly answered the question of if a monstrous dragon kept a giant spider as a pet.

The dragon's mouth had flickers of flames dancing about. It did not use its breath on the door. The spell trap waiting behind was not enough to kill the dragon, but in the small, enclosed area, it would be enough to hurt it. Its eyes darted around at the spider. Another came running out of the room.

"Oh no." Vakandi's voice lowered as he spoke. "There's a nest! Someone left the window open."

His feet shook the floor beneath her, but she tossed her purple mushroom powder on herself to go invisible and took off running to the dragon. Getting a single attack would not work, but multiple could. There was a small paste in her coat. With enough heat put on it, it would explode, it was her original plan to stop the dragon. She summoned her flying staff and flew up to the stalactites and smeared them on the first ones. The speed of the staff was too slow as the dragon crisped up one spider already. There was nothing quick about flying. She skipped the next and splattered the one after, circling around it. More spiders came out, but now she needed one to make it up here. The paste emptied on the third spot, right above the barracks doorway. Balancing on her staff, she pulled her knife out and cut her hand and smeared a dark red handprint next to the paste. She glided back behind the dragon, completely visible, and wrapped her hand with a bandage. The creatures of the Black Forest are always driven by the smell of blood.

By the time she finished her descent down, the spiders were already up on the ceiling. Their sticky white web extended out as they reached for her blood. She smiled as her simple hunting trick still worked.

Even though the Black Forest spiders were easy to deal with, seeing six of them full grown in this area meant something had been feeding them. Possibly a dragon who had "failed" to kill them in case a hero came to kill him. He wanted her to open the door and die to the spiders.

"Thank you!" Vakandi shouted, then launched small fireballs out of his mouth and shot at the grouped-up spiders. Sisal had expected a stream of fire, but of course, the dragon was worried about breaking his cave.

The third fireball hit the first dynamite paste right above the door. Its explosion heat gave way to the next one, and it triggered across into the last one perfectly. The roof shook and the stone spears fell down and hit Vakandi Foreldri in his head, shoulders, and back. She put the staff away in the bag and drew her blade. She forged a spell of ice to coat the weapon, cursing she did not study more death magic. Life magic was the counter to the monsters of the Black Forest. There had been no hints of him being a Giver of Life. Next dragon she fought, she would be well-versed in all the magic types to make the fight easier.

A frozen mist emitted off her blade as she stabbed into Vakandi's tail, where it connected to his main body. She called upon her bracelet shield. It still had one charge left. The hit came, but not from the tail, but from ahead like a horse kick, destroying the shield. Vakandi's heavy foot smashed the shield and stuttered with shield impact. Sandwiched between a clawed foot and a spikey tail, she growled and charged at the swinging tail. It hit her harder than expected. Her blade flew out of her hand as fast as her breath, as she smacked into his scales. It took her entire focus to grab onto the small deep ruby color plate. Air swished by. She pulled out a knife, coughing, and attacked. The blade bounced off, leaving the smallest dent where it had landed.

Catching her breath, and the dirt from the explosion floating in the air, she swore to not give up. She thought of her family, of her lover, of her commander, and of her country. The spell of ice summoned again and lined her small knife. The spell cracked and splintered as she pierced into a joining point of the scales, going at an angle to dig under and into his flesh.

The roar from Vakandi was so loud that her ears rang nonstop, as if twenty cannons fired next to her head. The tail moved and tightened around her like a python snake.

"I thought you finished doing this pointless fighting." The dragon's voice came to her mind, not through her ears. All the words spewed out heat and her mind burned. Searing the letters S-T-O-P in her mind. If she had time, she would chisel out "NO" into his own tail. With her precious time, she called on another ice spell to crackle along her blade. Raised it up to stab and felt herself lift with her blade.

His claws pinched her belt and flicked her into the air. At the peak of her flight, she twisted around, seeing the ground below her and a deadly, evergreen decorated stalactite pointing up. Panicking, she flicked her wrist, praying the merchant had it wrong on the shield charge counter. Three flicks later, her momentum put her hair's breadth above the stalactite. Before smashing to her death, the small breath she had caught earlier escaped again. She wriggled and twisted, pushed on the claw foot grasping her, even with her teeth she tried to bite down into the cretin, but none of her attacks did anything. A golden eye locked with hers. In the black iris, she saw herself fearful of what she had done to doom Vakfored.

"Skjöldur." A bauble of light from the evergreen garland on a nearby stalactite floated up to her, growing larger and engulfed her. The air was ambient, the light a gentle yellow haze, but Vakandi Foreldri's eyes pierced through crystal clear. His foot let go of her, and she floated in the air.

"You will sit in there for a bit to prevent getting you - or myself," he grumbled, "hurt further. I need to step back into my cavern to calm down."

His colossal form stomped off, his head standing tall enough to almost scrape the moonstone archway. A proud swat came from his tail. "You will listen to my story, Sisal, warrior and leader of Vakfored."

10. LUNCH

The bauble bubble floated to the ground after Vakandi left the room. Sisal poked the encasing with her finger and knife. It only moved it forward. Stepping forward, the whole thing shifted and rolled around her. The first few times she slid down the edge of the ball. After a few more steps of practice, she had the hang of the hazy bubble that encased her and roamed around. She would have to do a sprint to get over some bumps or piles of gold. If she ran too hard, she would launch off like it was a ramp going further than she wanted and end up spinning around in the bauble. Pacing around the table at the Guild of Adventures typically burned off the jitters and cleared her cloudy thoughts. Running around gold and dead spider bodies only made the stress worse. The hazy vision of the bubble felt too realistic a representation of her mind.

Vakandi's last words bothered her. She came here to slay him. Doing so would not make her a leader of Vakfored. Being a Queen was the last thing she wanted. The crown was only another wall around her, trapping her from what she wanted, freedom, and try being in a play or see an orchestra. A quick glance at the paper in her bag to confirm the reward. Lots of gold and a sword, which she already got. Nothing about being sworn as the next ruler. Not that she had to worry about that in her current situation. She did not even worry about her death anymore.

If Vakandi wanted her dead, he had plenty of chances and kept to his promise. Though the burning letters of "STOP" still itched, and guessing by the magical agreement, did not count as harm. She would rather not find the crossing point of what pain he could do her before the laws of magic declared he went too far.

She wandered about the gold cavern, running up and down the hills of gold. The bubble did not let her actually touch anything, not a single coin fell from the pile as she rolled down them. After being launched a second time, she kept a far distance from the cavern entrance in fear of going down the mountainside. The bubble could not fit the barracks where the kónguló came from. The door - and the window- were wide open, but no spiders came out, and the rats ran away. Exploring the rest of the cavern showed there was not much more to it than when she initially snuck in here before sunrise. There were pillars showcasing the art and pottery. Not a single bookshelf lined the place. She stopped by the moonstone archway in the middle of the entrance, wobbling for a moment while looking at the gold piles. She put her hands on her hips, shaking her head. "Knowledge is value, but he doesn't write it down."

"That is Vakfored's job." He interrupted her and pinched his claws near the bubble. "And it's impossible for me to turn the pages of a book. I end up ripping them up with time. Fortunately, I am a dragon, with an excellent memory."

"What are you going to do with me?" His page tearing claws could easily tear her apart.

"I swore on all the magics that I would not harm you. I will continue to tell my story."

The longest winded dragon in existence, and his words brought her relief. "So, you can't harm me while I am in this?"

"I summoned the skjöldur, I can destroy it. I left because I lost my temper."

Nothing about this dragon made sense the more she listened to him. A dragon should be angry and greedy. He filled this cave filled with trea-

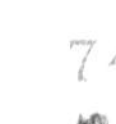

sure, but none of it was his. "Bards from traveling lands talk about dragon hoards filled with gold, weapons, armor, potions, and scrolls." Sisal stretched her arms out. "You have baubles literally hanging from stalactites that illuminate the place. Even plain evergreens wrapped around the stalagmites. Besides the gold - which isn't yours - and the moonstone, you only have historical non-magical items. Are these dragon tales only lavished for our entertainment?"

"History has value. Plus, those are truly magical evergreens. They still have their smell after a century of being wrapped up."

"You are dodging the question."

"The stories aren't lavished. I have valuable elixirs." For once, he was on the defensive side. "I know of a dragon who lined a hallway with what was the latest of times armor. They had collected it by killing multiple intruders over the years."

"You don't get many intruders?"

"At one point there was a bad influx of them, but generally not. Most people who come here are my guests."

The gold cavern had three armor sets filled with bone dust. She circled it twice to confirm. She did not recall armor in the hearth area. It was unlikely he only had three unwanted visitors. "You hardly have any armor. Did you eat that with the intruders?"

"I did. Swallowed it quickly to avoid the dried leather and metal taste."

Her heart stopped. What she had said was half a joke. His tales never mentioned him eating anyone. Her grandparents said he did. "Um, it causes indigestion?"

"I should have just burnt them. I actually got heartburn from their oiliness. Wretched things slicked back their fur." Vakandi Foreldri coughed and his tail swatted around. "Oh, the memory ruined my appetite, but I should still make you lunch. The chickens laid eggs."

There were chickens in a dragon hoard. This was the poorest dragon of all history. He lied about not being able to turn the pages of a book if he could crack eggs. The library of Vakfored beamed with tomes, books, and ballads. She spent lunch breaks there studying about the warfare of other countries, and the recent technology for Vakfored. After hearing a bard play at the tavern some incredible music, she realized she had never heard a song from Vakfored. Music was the heart of a culture as much as dance, art, and stories. Once Vakandi was gone and she got her payment from finishing this mission, she wanted to travel to hear a variety of music. To learn to play an instrument like the bards. To become skilled enough to make a melody to go with the song woven in on the cloth that sat in her bag. "What killed the music of Vakfored? What ended the Age of Ballads?"

"Cats. A traveling musical group came in and it was never the same."

11. THE VACATION

The orc Queen of Vakfored had a dwarf whispering in her ear. He did not work the mines, but of the stone laying and architecture. Because of that, they styled their beards trimmed and short. This one had more silver and copper bands on his fingers than on his beard. He had as many bands as the Queen had jewels and magical illusions placed around her to make her glow. The light glistening off her sharp tucks. An intimidating look for anyone who was not Vakandi. The current annoying, repetitive conversation continued on between Vakandi and her. It was the same words he exchanged with the King before her, and the other royals and all the way back to the guild masters when the problem first arose.

"Shadow of my Sun," spoke Queen Nargol. Her tone was not in reverence, but one of stubbornness. "Why do we need to waste our resources? You've been doing a wonderful job guarding the city."

"It's not a waste - but a necessity! Every city near the mountains has a dam built on the river as a precaution."

"Not every city has you. You are our personal guard."

"You won't appreciate what I do until I am gone."

The dwarf raised his hand to speak. The Queen nodded to let him talk. "I believe we do. We heard you thumping in the dark in your cave.

You are so cautious in not burning the Golden Essence gold, or crushing it, they paid our guild to construct you that arch out of the moonstone. That took up half the stone!"

The moonstone had proven really useful. Before the piles of gold showed up, he would just create some fires in his cave to avoid stepping into all the stalagmites in the dark. Or just stay inside until the sun rose so he could see. The Vakfored created elevators, chimes of a light sound, and alleviated a heavy broken heart with potions from the moonstone. The asteroid must have fallen before Vakandi even settled into the land. "I do appreciate the gift."

"Excellent!" Queen Nargol clapped. "Then there is nothing more to talk about. We will shift our *normal* production of stasis potions to make the dragon healing elixirs."

He growled, annoyed at their lack of listening and understanding. They thought it was fine because they gave him potions to heal quickly, then he can do it all again, like the pain did not hurt. The elixirs helped, but it was only a temporary solution to the entire problem. There was a saying that if you said the same thing a thousand times, maybe it was not the listener who was not learning, but the speaker. Sometimes the hatchlings need to learn on their own and he needed to learn to stop hovering. "No. There is another matter I wish to advise on. You need to build walls and a watchtower. As the city of Vakfored grows, the world becomes smaller and more threatened by your presence."

"Yes, yes, yes," The queen exasperated. "As you have said many times. We hear you. When it becomes a problem, we will address it."

"If that happens, it's too late! You could lose hundreds of your citizens. Act before it's too late."

The Vakfored court unified in a sigh at hearing the same speech their grandparents heard. Vakandi Foreldri failed to educate his hatchlings. He had said the same thing over hundreds of times and they still did not act. He saved them from floods on multiple occasions, another avalanche, and his presence kept beasts at bay. Maybe it was time he said it differently.

"You mentioned before how you wanted to expand your farmlands. I can't take up the protection over there and keep up with my regular patrol. But if you wish to do it on your own, feel free." Vakandi offered. He almost felt as cold as ice with the words. This had to happen. He could not flap his wings and fly over the city's land forever. He had his own life to live at one point. They needed to grow up. This little adventure out on the farmlands would be good for both of them.

Those around the court finished their gossiping among themselves. The dwarf stopped scratching his short beard. "The soil there is rich, not much salt. Alright, we will start building farms. After you do a cleansing of any monsters."

"I did it yesterday. But still, I suggest you prepare yourself. You never know what nest of worms you will find. You should prepare a guard on the perimeter."

The Queen clapped in excitement. "About time this happened. None of the other city-nations have to wait on a dragon's permission to expand. Let's have lunch and discuss building the twelfth ring around the city. With the new farmland further in the south, we can now expand for all our new settlers." She completely ignored his last bit of advice about adding a guard. Even Queen Nargol did not have a guard around her. The city was in such peace she could freely roam without ever being threatened.

Vakandi tilted his head, exhausted from repeating himself, and flew up and out of the main circle. The stone bricks rattled beneath his feet as he lifted into the air. But because of the magic imbued in them, they shifted back to their spots to continue to show a circle pattern of red and white bricks. Any other dragon would see it as a challenge to destroy this city. The children started hitting the drums as he left. Other flutes and percussion instruments played as the meeting with the dragon ended. Normally the music sounded longing and sad, but today there were fewer flutes and more trumpets playing instead of the string instruments. There was a bit of a pep in the beat. His presence was becoming taxing on the

Vakfored. They needed a vacation from him, but they were not ready.

No matter how many times he told them, they would not research attack spells, create armor, or weapons. They had basic traps and hunting bows, even a few carving knives. Not enough to stand up against a genuine threat. Like an increase of bogga bears in the bog, he had to deal with it the other day as they chased off a farmer. While he handled with that, he heard the Queen pray at her hearth for an early release of a book she had been waiting on. The farmer even returned to the bog the next day, with only a shovel to dig up peat moss. Zero traps, not even a dagger to defend himself with if more bogga bears showed up. No one felt like any threat was permanent or real.

Maybe, with one more sweep around the land with a wider parameter, burn a werewolf, vampire, or minotaur would keep the city safe for a bit. Then a long overdue trip to see the ocean. It had been a few centuries since he took some time to himself.

Because Vakfored burned their dead, there was not a zombie problem. Instead, there were a few fire spirits in the west. The north had a few small yetis pushing near Vakandi's cave again. There was also a famished werewolf in the Black Forest in the east. The last spot he visited was in the south, where the farms were expanding. An odd smell was up in the air as he passed over a gathering of harvesters dressed in black leather, preparing some instruments. Near a glade of flattened grass laid some bones next to a tall collection of large stones. Upon further inspection, it revealed they were bones of sheep and bison, neatly laid out and organized by size. The woolen fur was gone, but scraps of meat remained. Goat bones hid among the sheep ones. The smell did not match death, but of an animal marking its territory. Vakandi's eyes wandered over the plain's green grass to where it turned into plump husks of summer wheat and corn. Not too far were more herding sheep, calmly grazing on the grass. Beyond them came the sound of music from a nearby set of harvesters. The music was a little too lively. There was some odd magic in the music too, as if it was using the common house cat meow and roars. Someone struck a washboard to even create a purring sound.

Vakandi Foreldri shook his head. At one point, listening to the music of Vakfored had been a joy. They would sing lyrics together, dance, and laugh. The noise coming from the harvesters had a bit too much of a modern style music to it. The city today did not appreciate the true artists of the past.

He flew off to the southeast, away from the racquet. Giving some distance to Vakfored would be the best. They could ultimately learn to build some farms, a dam, and some walls to protect themselves. He could finally get some rest without worrying about them every day and night. They were not his blood kin, but did the other dragons struggle this much and this long in raising their hatchlings? A question he would have to ask his parents, but they had settled deep into a mountain and talking to them had become as painful as ice slamming into his back. This trip was about relaxing, not worrying about a city.

It did not take long for him to find the ocean. It was summer, the smell of kelp and salt strong in the air. In centuries past, he would come here and stretch his wings. He would play with a bit of magic to see how deep he could split the ocean and find the bottom floor. The fish would flop about desperately looking for water. Instead, they found the hot mouth of a dragon. Fresh salty fish! Now, he did the old trick, and he was a bit out of practice. If anyone watched, they would see an embarrassed dragon get closer to the shore to part the waters and catch the fish. He successfully caught a massive fish, one at least as tall as an orc. With the small snack in his belly, Vakandi flew further across the ocean until he found the other continent. The sun had set as he listened to the waves splash. No meetings listening to complaints about how things should be, with no thanks for what had been done. No village proofing a place because they would not develop a defense plan. This night would be free of thoughts of the Vakfored. These were the moments he took for granted. He really missed roaming around and seeing new cliffs, smelling fresh scents, hearing unfamiliar sounds, and resting. Actually, resting too, not just for the six hours of sleep the people gave him.

With this freedom, there was so much that he wanted to do that he could not rest! It had been a while since he had met another dragon. Maybe he could have fun with them. Meeting another one would always turn into fights though, they usually worried about their turf. Up on the coast in the rising moonlight, the lights of another city grew. A bit of fire broke off from the city, small like a few torches sneaking in and out of the woods nearby. The fully risen quarter moon glistened on the water's surface when the group of people vanquished their fires. Their presence near Vakandi was an obvious message to their plans.

The air warmed drastically, as if magic was being channeled. Vakandi braced himself, growing a shield of magic around his skin. The people would have been better off using scrolls and sneaking around, not jingling up in armor and charging spells. They were so precautious of his arrival that they forgot to think about their own presence.

"People, words go further than magic when saying hello." He offered the advice to them.

The people did not agree as a fireball launched toward his face. It always had to be the face. He blew out a puff of wind at it, disturbing the water tides nearby.

12. THE TALISMAN

At the bottom of the bubble, Sisal laid there with her feet elevated above her head. "You can cut to the chase. You ate the people, and they lived in fear of you."

"I did. But they did not. If anything, they became more determined." Vakandi stated. "I had not finished the story before you rudely interrupted."

The bubble sat between a pile of gold. With a tap of her foot, she could rock back and forth briefly. As much as the imprisonment prevented her from doing any plans, she thought it was a lot more comfortable than the chairs by the hearth. "I don't get the point of this story. Like before, you are avoiding answering my questions."

"Apparently they don't teach history anymore." Before she could refute back, he continued. "That vacation I did worsen the relationship I had with Vakfored more than I could ever imagine. I had not been ready then. I am still not ready to say what happened later, and what I should have said before."

The last words made her jump up, careful to not shake the bubble too much, and looked up to the monstrous dragon. Her hands flexed on the side, but no weapon but her voice would help her now. The entire nation believed he was an expert at avoiding their cries, but she would get an answer now. "I wanted to know what happened to the music of Vakfored and you gave me a roundabout answer of sheep and a farmer. Then your fishing trip. Not really answering why we don't sing outside of funerals."

"A city loses its voice but gains its independence." He saw the confusion on her face and continued. "The answer is not a short one of a 'Yes', 'No', or even 'K'. There is more to understanding why it happened. This is not a story in a footnote. It is why you have the statues you do in your city. All because I looked away from raising you. I thought you could do it on your own. I thought I could handle it."

His words made her stop fidgeting. His inflection matched those of a human when they feel regret. It's a good thing she made him swear on all the magic about leaving once he finished his long-winded tales. If he had the choice, he would try to recount every detail of every day until then that it would be faster to live it.

She would have music sheets and choreographed dances if he did. Even the music he considered too modern, pinpointed to instrument and style type, if only he listened more.

"The sun is starting its descent. How convenient we start part of the story that leads to my own." He grumbled more under his breath.

It was past noon, and she was full because of the four eggs he served her with more soup. The items passed in and out of the bubble with his command. Magical abilities equated with the strengths of the person or being controlling it. If someone is swift, they are strong in the wind, but if they are sleek and quick, they will lean into the cold ice magic. Sisal's strength was that of the earth, but using the earth on a red fire dragon would be foolish. Her ice magic was weak, which is why she packed so many spells in her bag. Vakandi easily controlled the bubble. Transparency could be Vakandi Foreldri's strongest magic after fire.

If he was truly that transparent, that meant everything told so far was the truth. From the ceramics, the plate hearth blessing, the Golden Essence, Engill's Perigon, and even the song on the tapestry. All of it was proof that he listened to her request and was explaining what ruined Vakfored's music. She interrupted him. All this time she was not receptive to his story, she had to try to listen. "Sorry. Could you please continue and tell me what happened?"

The dragon chuckled, pinched around the bauble and put her near an evergreen wrapped stone and a dead spider's body. Next to the evergreen hung a wide necklace with multiple teeth weaved in and out, the yellowing on the roots proof they were not fake. The clasp of a gold belt buckle sat in the middle of the black leather cord. He put his head down near her. "Little Sisal, you have the choice to leave." His eyes glanced over at the entrance, a small bit of smoke spilling out of nostrils. He looked back and his head nudged the necklace. "Or to stay and listen."

A small smile stretched across her lips as she crossed her legs settling in to take in every detail Vakandi Foreldri offered of the Vakfored history.

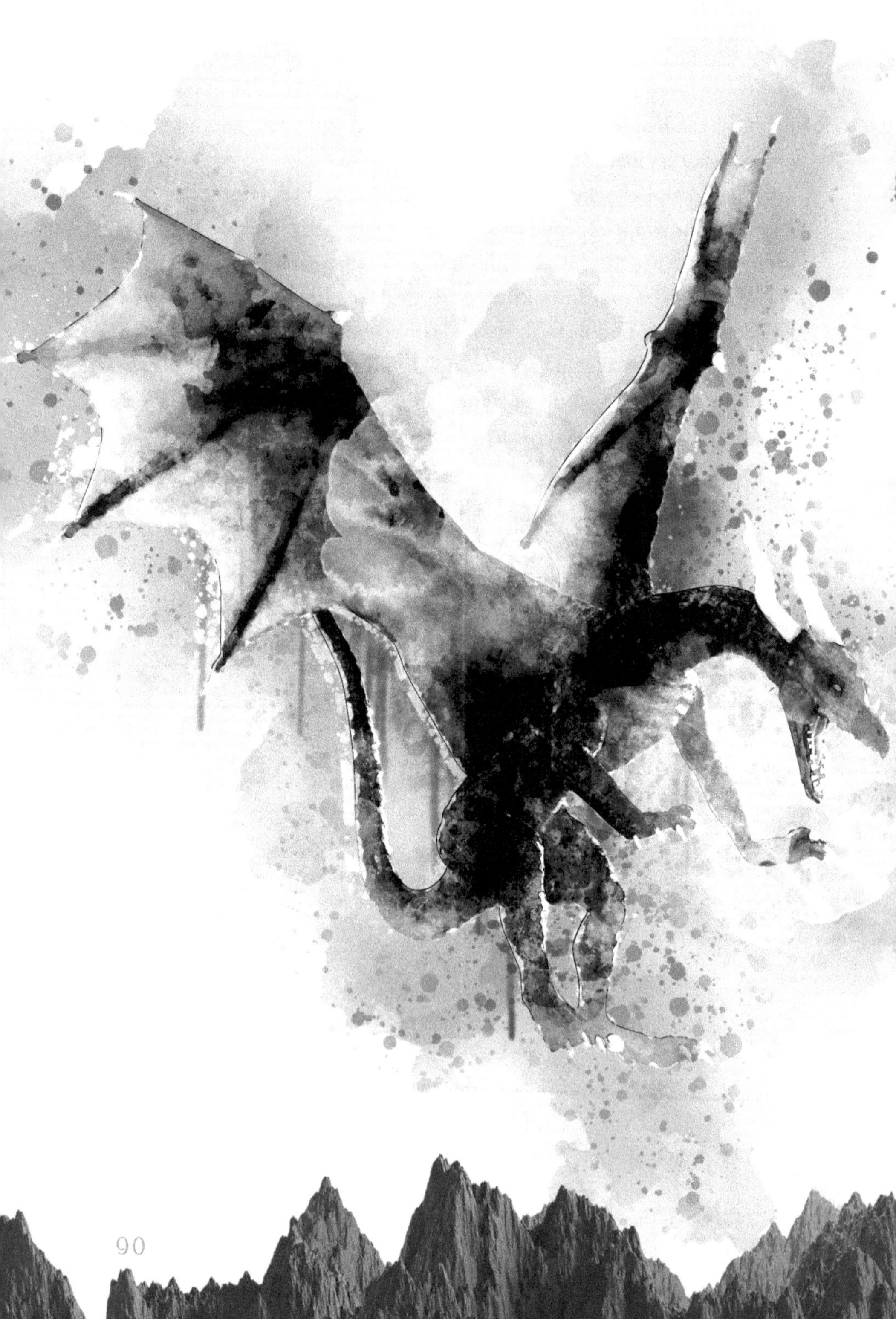

13. THE CATS

The fireball attack from the people in the woods tickled. With how weak it was, Vakandi attempted to say hello again and to have them come out and hang out on the beach. "What a warm welcome. I definitely prefer that over an icy one."

They did not appreciate the joke, but returned a response filled with bitter sharp edges. A volley of icicles pricked at his magical shield. "My, my, you at least listen to what I say. Is there a way I could have you talk to-"

A spear of ice charged at him and he ordered the fire to melt it, but still he took a step back, his foot landing in the warm ocean water. Blood boiled in his chest at the insult. This is how the people always lived, destruction and greed of anything more powerful than them. They hated the idea of being weak. They were only ants in his eyes.

A sword whacked at his leg, a spear jabbed, and a paladin prayed as they punched at Vakandi. Their pure faith in believing in what they did was right. So did the Vakfored and Vakandi. With a kick of his foot, they were all knocked away. He blew fire near them to scare them. The paladin shook off the hit and created a divine shield, leading at least six of his allies as they screamed and charged forward. They were unbroken. The mages and druids stayed in the back, preparing even more spells.

Vakandi stomped his feet and roared in their direction. Fire spewing out between his teeth. The numbers of his attackers diminished. They had not come armed enough to deal with Vakandi Foreldri.

They could not prepare in such a small amount of time. A massive beast landed on their shore and they went to defend as soon as possible. They were not invading his vacation. He invaded their home like a were-beast from the Black Forest.

The wind gathered under his wings, and he pushed up into the air, the water on the shore retreating from the force. His gust spread the fire to the bushes nearby. The sparks jumped and branched out. It had been a party of ten people coming at him, and they were not ready to take on a dragon as old as him. They did nothing wrong.

He did.

He should not have left home without setting a few spell traps to keep Vakfored safe. A giant beast like him could show up and destroy everything they had strived for. At least this city could defend their ocean and land fronts with its boats and walls. Their banner of a four-legged scaly creature with long digging claws was threatening, reminding him of a certain ice beast. Certainly, they had cannons to attack with as well. Vakfored's banner was an open door with an image of Vakandi embracing them in a hug.

He used a bit of magic and snuffed out the fire before taking off into the sky. There was no point in apologizing for his actions. They would not listen to a dragon, friendly or not. The moon shined over the ocean waves as he returned to his land and domain. Not too far from the coast, the waves became disrupted as something much larger than a fish moved beneath the surface. The water gurgled and ice floated to the top, a threatening message to a fire dragon. In the dark, he could not see the beast, but with how easily it froze the ocean, it had to be as old as him. With fear motivating him, he picked up speed to get home faster. A similar ancient monster could appear and walk into Vakfored right now. Eating all the people that lived there, hurting the city he fostered. He needed to land in the central ring and make sure they were safe.

The colorful lights from the city lit up the night sky as if it was the new year. The city saw him leave during the day. With his return at night and their lack of watchtowers, they had no way of knowing he returned. They celebrated that their tyrannical dragon left. Originally, he thought of stopping by to check up on them, but with the light magic and even fireworks going up in the sky, he would only dampen their mood. To avoid getting hit by a firework, he skirted around near the eleventh ring of the city, but he hoped one person would look up. For someone to make one illusion of a dragon and have it dancing.

Instead, the light magic made illusions of those darn fur-balls the people liked to keep as pets. Cats pounced along, chasing balls of yarn in the sky. Cats could not even naturally fly! There was a design of a stripped tabby curled up, a leopard one grooming itself, even one sitting still flicking its tail. Such tame creatures compared to a dragon. Once no longer distracted by the blinding lights, he heard the music. It had no rhythm. It went slowly, then fast, then a hybrid of both with cymbals making a third one in the background. A roar emitted out, the sound of a creature from the plains far in the south.

A traveling troupe arrived in the city, playing a performance very late into the night. Distracting the people of the hardships they had to deal with. To enjoy a night of fun filled with music, chasing around, and food. They dedicated even the theaters and taverns to playing the ruckus they called modern music.

Vakandi Foreldri closed his eyes, feeling forcefully pleased the closer he got to the city. Under the illusionary magic, there came a distinct scent. One that brought comfort, calm, and would put the weak minded to sleep. Like his people.

They were being tempted by a hallucination spell. Once he noticed it, he could hear his Vakfored crying under the roars and clanging music. More than one monster moved into his city while he went out to relax. The magic and the annoying music all lined up with a single type of monster. A troupe of werelions were ravishing in the city. They flooded the theaters and amphitheaters, making sure everyone heard the music, but no one heard the truth.

The Vakfored had only designed two spots for Vakandi Foreldri to set down; the inner ring and the out by the funeral pyre in the southeast on the sixth through tenth ring. He landed in the center of the city. Smoking plants laid about the streets to distribute the mind-bending magic. It had the same tannin smell as out on the farms. Couches from all the nearby houses and Queen's palace sat in the street. Werelions with their manes greased back flicked their tails as they lounged on the leather couches in their own black leather clothing. Golden belts, bracelets, and earrings reflected in the light. The lioness of the clan hunted down the people to only lick their paws once done hunting.

Vakandi let out a cry, fire erupting from his mouth into the sky, the small sparks falling down on the city. It did nothing to wake the people from the illusion and not realizing the theatrical play they were in was not an act. A few werelions ran inside the buildings. Vakandi made a mental note to hunt them soon, but first he had to wake his people. The werelions near the circle hissed and growled up at him, taunting him with their clawed, stained, fur paws, but too afraid to approach him. His own claws glistened in the city light. He fanned the air with his wings, calling on purer winds to arrive in and force the hallucinogen smoke elsewhere. It would not be enough. Only the few surviving dwarves, humans, and orcs nearby broke from the drug.

His dug his claws deep into the magical bricks, digging a bit until he felt the earth. He willed it to awaken and shake the city. The connection to the earth became comforting, a place of home. Images of playing in the sand as a hatchling came to mind. He could dig up all the bricks and play in it.

Another roar erupted from his chest and he shook the city in sound and ground. The image of comforts of the past were being created by the psychedelic magic. Cowardly tricks played by the souls who served the moon and its illusions of the night. They hid at noon, blended as people on the outskirts of the city in the farm fields. They waited until the fire dragon, a servant of the sun, left the city to attack and make their dens. As long as Vakandi focused on it, he knew there was a hallucinogen in place. The pitiful cats who ran inside houses earlier returned, pulling out couches and chairs from the nearby homes.

Two lionesses charged him down on all four paws, roaring as they pounced. Their leather clothes failing to hide the tuffs of fur sticking out in places.

"Let's play cat versus mouse, little kitties." Vakandi Foreldri hissed.

The words had not finished leaving his mouth as the werelions scratched and clawed at the couches. They screeched back as they gathered. Their whiskers, noses, and paws stained, yet their teeth remained pristine white and their claws razor sharp as they frolicked on their hind legs. The largest of the werelions landed nearby, his mane spiked up in the center with oil, grinning as he approached the great dragon. He skipped and pranced, and swung its tail around in one hand. "Big old dragon wants to join Sir Androlemew Leon of Webbton?"

Confident fur-ball, that name was probably not even real. They may have numbers more than the coastal city when they attacked Vakandi. However, the werelions were nothing. "Tell me, how many people have died tonight? Or am I to believe that only a few couches got damaged, and you only lavished on the sheep on the farms?"

Sir Androlemew stopped swinging his tail as his eyes dashed over the other cats. "You aren't here to make a claim to this city?"

Vakandi swung his tail, pointing at the closest banner that was not shredded by the werelions. The outline of a dragon embracing a city. "You came into my home, partied up, and played this horrible music to hide the screams of my people. I am here to devour the intruders."

The growling of the werelions stopped. The dragon was not here to eat the people. Swiftly, the werelions scattered around upon realizing they were the target of the apex predator.

"Look at all the little mice run and the big cat wanted to snack."

Words were the only way Vakandi could vent his temper. He wanted to burn everything down for what was going on. To kill those who harmed his hatchlings. However, any fire attack in the city would harm the people more than the werelions.

Sir Androlemew quickly darted inside a house, abandoning his pride. The others were not as fast and lost with the sudden abandonment. Vakandi bit and swallowed the stragglers whole. Three down, and too many to go. As he hunted, the hallucinogen spell faded, making the screams in the city worse and the growls of the werelions desperate. Panic and fear grew to such levels that the illusion spell could do nothing on the people any more. It was still too late; the damage had been done.

The werelions swiped at his nose, scratching it. The pain was nothing like what was happening in heart hearing his hatchlings cry. Vakandi used a claw to stab at each window where he smelled or heard a werelion, chasing the monsters out. His people cowered in fear. Only a few people stood up to the monsters. They only had kitchen knives and hunting bows to defend themselves. A few miners used their pickaxes, but on a whole his hatchlings could not protect themselves. He should have never left without preparing them. He could have trained them better.

He found Sir Androlemew down by the tenth ring near the funeral pyre of Engill's Perigon in time before the sun broke the horizon. Vakandi did not give him the luxury of a burning to greet the sun and day. Instead, he snatched up Sir Androlemew and played and tossed him around the same way the werelions treated his people and banner. Vakandi lost many people, his Vakfored that night.

Vakfored sent too many souls to be greeted back into the cycle of magic and the world. Even as they prepared to send the souls off, the scars on the living cut just as deep. Many people had been bit during the werelion attack and forced into quarantine. They could not partake in saying goodbye to their loved ones or to embrace the next day at risk of turning when the moon rose at night. Every time a chimed played, a drum, a flute, or guitar, those who survived shivered and feared of being caught in the spell again. It reminded them of how they could not be part of the sendoff cycle.

The medics and mages treated the quarantine with death magic and plants from the Black Forest. It took time, but they found a cure, even if moons later. The werelions left their mark on the city. Even centuries later, Vakfored still depended on the plants, and thankfully they did or else the city of would be only werelions and no people.

The thought of the place being overrun by those beasts made Vakandi's stomach turn and his chest hurt. The healers and Queen Nargol offered to look him over, but he said nothing as he flew off to Black Forest hunting all the monsters he could find. He flew to the farm, patrolling it daily. He found the corpses of the sheep and goat in the plains, burning them for his foolish mistake in ignoring the signs of another predator sneaking into his nest.

The werelions attacking Vakfored had been his fault. If only he did not fly off in anger and selfishness. He should have forced his hatchlings to learn how to attack and defend. Instead, he continued to lavish in their musical and artistic abilities. The way they constantly created in the world fed his soul and strengthened his mind while weakening them. They had not grown since being a small pack of ill-prepared refugees. The Vakfored could have built a dam by now, but they chose not to listen. They argued against the idea of a wall and watchtower every time. They only wanted him as their shield and sword.

Vakandi Foreldri needed a plan to help the city become a nation on its own, in case anything ever happened to him.

14. TEA TIME

Silence filled the gold chamber. All the stories of Vakandi Foreldri showed off his pride and power. This was the first of how he lowered his head. Sisal's finger traced the shell of the bubble she was in, starting above her head and pausing at the halfway point. The equilibrium where she could move forward if she pushed, or roll back if she stepped backward. No one could maintain equilibrium for long at the peak of the curve. She started whistling the song her father used to sing to her when younger. Her voice was a bit raspier. A simple tune from another country, of knights, mages, and druids, of life and the courage it takes to continue on. The eyes of Vakandi narrowed as he listened, but he did not tell her to stop. When she sung the last line, she mockingly clapped herself to break the tension in the air.

His claw tapped next to the bubble. "Beautifully sung. It's not from here."

"How can you tell?"

"The Vakfored always embraced death, singing highly of it, not hiding it or seeing it as an end."

"I should add to the lyrics then."

The bubble popped around her, and she fell down to the ground. "Let me get you a pen and paper."

She followed, surprised by his offer. "Wait, I thought you said you didn't record anything down!"

The chuckle emitted from his throat. "I don't because I can't hold the paper. That's the truth. If I could, I could only write the story as the guardian of Vakfored. I could never truly say what the people of Vakfored lived through."

Her hand shifted to her sword. She had come here to kill him because of tales her grandparents told. They instilled a mindset of hating Vakandi upon her. All this time, she saw the dragon as an oppressor. Now, she looked at the dragon banner and wonder why she saw it as a vulture, not as a shield with wings spread out protecting the young city. The only prey he hunted on were the monsters which hunted the city and the bison which were set aside for him. Instead of writing lyric songs, she wanted to write the story he told. To keep the words the same as he had told them, without the influence of her as a narrator changing them.

It was fortunate the great Vakandi out powered her in their fight in order to tell this story. This day would have been different if she could have come with an army or a group of other adventurers. A strong enough group with her as the leader could have slain him, then they would have erased the history of Vakandi completely. That process was already happening. There was no information about Bedruk and Vakandi being friends. He saved the Vakfored multiple times, and they made him a place to land so he could visit. Her grandparents taught her the inner circle was where the royalty had to be ready to listen to Vakandi's demands. They built the Guild of Adventurers nearby to face him off with a group of mercenaries.

She paused by the table in the back cavern, looking out at the entrance. The shadows were growing since noon as the sun started down toward the mountains. It was the afternoon. She came to the cave to kill him. If she did, she would be tossing a shield for the nation aside. If he was a friend, she would feel worse about making him swear on all the magics. But a friend would have acted, not betrayed them. He had to tell her the full, truthful story. He stretched the truth that it became confusing. Or was it her research and what her family taught her that made his truth feel clouded?

"The barracks can sleep multiple people," she said. "I could have come here with a true adventuring troop."

"Yes." Vakandi stood under the moonstone arch. For the first time today, he said nothing else.

She needed more. Everything between their exchange had been transparent so far. But if there was one lie, everything else had to be to be taken with a grain of salt, and she would be back mentally where she was yesterday. She wanted this peaceful, beautiful truth that Vakfored and Vakandi lived side by side with only minor bickering. If it was false, then they had suffered for generations under his rule.

"Is the rumor of allowing one pure soul to enter the cave a lie?"

He turned and looked back at the entrance. His tail pointed toward the barracks. "Multiple souls can enter. I once had a hundred Vakfored in this cave. Purity... I don't understand that. A soul can be pure by growing flowers, and by burning crops as long as the actor believes they are in the right without a shadow of a doubt."

"You did not create the rumor?"

"Sisal, do you know if I have talked to the people?"

She crossed her arms, holding herself back from saying more. He had to stay on this subject. "Don't deflect the question."

Vakandi walked over and put his head down. "I suggested against that rumor being made. I believe my story will reveal who did it. They only did it to buy me time... to give me a chance to change my mind."

Her shoulders slumped, but the tension remained. He still could not give her a simple answer. It could be a long complex answer like why there is no music of the Vakfored, all because of the scar the werelions left. The song her dad taught her was in private, even when her mom was not around. If she kept listening to Vakandi, he would reveal the truth, marking her mission complete. Then, he had to leave Vakfored because she forced him. It's not that they needed him as a shield to hunt werelions anymore. She could do that. There were worse monsters and nations in the world than yetis and the Vakfored could use his aid. Forcing him to leave could be the worst idea ever for Vakfored. If she walked out of the cave now, she would never know the definitive answer for his betrayal against his hatchlings.

She could appease Vakfored and listen to the rest. If he lied, it would be the right option and save Vakfored from fear and get avenge for his cruelty that her great grandparents lived through. She could also choose to run out of the cave and save their guardian.

Not every adventurer would be foolish like her and listen to the pure soul rumor - or a dragon. Everyone would question her why she failed and survived her mission. They would see her as a coward and no one would know the ultimate reason as to why the guardian of Vakfored broke their relationship.

Smoke trickled near her legs. She looked back to see Vakandi's head resting nearby, puffing out bits at a time.

"It's early afternoon." He stated.

"Are we nearing the end of your tale? Vakfored has a lot of history." She did not want him to end. This had been a ludicrous request. In the magical swearing, he had to finish his stories. If the story remained unfinished, he did not need to go. There were more stories to tell.

The plated tail of the dragon swung around, thumping the ground. "I have sworn on all the magics to leave by sunset. We set the motions, like snow going down a mountain and turning into an avalanche, it can't be stopped."

She stepped around him, his eyes following her as she pointed to his largest scar on his back. "You stopped a few before."

"To protect Vakfored."

"Don't stop. If the world knew we had a dragon defending us, no one would come to threaten us. We could go back to being the cultural city you talked about. We can go back to having music!"

Vakandi's eyes closed. The moonstone creating a sheen on the dark red scales. "I hope you find the ability to make music, dance, theater, and art again. To not use magic only for war."

She kept her mouth shut, something her commanding officer wished happened more often. Vakfored needed more land to expand. They had drained the land here of resources. Trading could only yield so much.

The fire in the hearth was diminishing, and a chill crept across her skin. As if sensing it, Vakandi lumbered over and picked up a few logs from a stack and tossed it in. "Could you please help me and toss that all in the hearth? I won't be needing it anymore." Vakandi requested. He tapped a bin filled with sticks and papers. "This too."

Soot gathered on the items in the bin. The papers filled with charcoal sketches of him. From full bodies to head sketches. One of the portrait ones she stuffed inside her bag. He looked content in it. This morning she was here to stab a dragon. This afternoon she used a fire poker to put kindling in a fire to keep the fire dragon warm and saved art work of him. The pile dwindled as the dragon hummed behind her, thinking about what to say next.

After a while, she finally reached the bottom of the pile and discovered a journal buried in the ash. She flipped a few pages and paused. There were detailed instructions of rituals of creating a magical barrier. Potions for the land to create endless harvest, and powerful magical attacks that could wipe an entire army in one go. All of them had one thing in common: dragon parts. Even how the use of the blood could freeze time on certain plants so they never stop producing. The common written language filled the journal, with a few words spelled differently, but still translatable. All the spells and rituals could solve Vakfored's problems. It would bring back her original mission of hunting down a dragon.

She could spill Vakandi's blood to have more than the bloody handkerchief in her bag. She could ignore the stories he had told. Call him a monster again to make it easier.

She would lose Vakfored's history.

If she acted now, her honor would be a lie.

Her hands danced over the journal. The fire would easily destroy it and the information lost.

"That book is recent. From the War of Beasts. Surprised its pages have not crisped up with where it's located." The dragon peeked above her shoulder.

This book could save them in case something happened to Vakandi Foreldri. "It's looked down upon to burn books in Vakfored," she replied.

"Should I keep all the cookbooks that talk about the best way to serve humans, orcs, and dwarves?" His voice took on a light pitch.

Mocking or not, it would be equally disturbing if she found a recipe book here with that subject. "Dragons don't keep cookbooks. You eat everything with one bite. Like oily fur."

The dragon reached over to his giant cooking pot and scooped out the best soup she had ever tasted. "I wrote this recipe down. The base started with a mountain goat and turnips. Let's see." His claw pointed to across to the end of the hearth near the human sink, picking up a piece of paper, the one he promised to give her earlier. "Guess this can be kindling too."

"Stop!" The world had to know about that soup.

"Sisal, tell me, who decides what history should be written and saved? The ones you agree with?"

"History should always tell every side of the story." She stared at his claw, pinching the soup recipe near the flames.

"Then should we destroy both this recipe and that book so they can be lost, or save them? Should I say the best way to enjoy all species?"

A soup recipe was not the same as people's lives. "I don't like it, but we should save them."

His claw pointed up. "But what if they aren't facts and only theories? The recipe for nourishing the fields with dragon bones is completely correct, just like using fish or goat bones. But making a potion of immortality with my heart it would do no such thing. The shield spell would fail too."

He did not mention the facts on the dragon blood and freezing time. Though earlier he pointed out how it could be like a picture frame. She pointed an accusing finger at the soup recipe. "You could be lying about these rituals like you lied about writing on paper and not knowing where to find that recipe."

The lips stretched to reveal the dragon's sharp teeth. "Excellent observation. You don't know. You can take my truth, or not. You can take that book, or burn it. I'm not perfect, and you wanted something more than a soup recipe." He pointed a claw back at her. "That spell book is why the War of Beasts happened. They dreamed of these rituals and spells, of the dragon hoard that would make them rich and heroes back at home."

"They taught me that the War of Beasts happened because of you. I was told you attacked their home."

"I did. The night the werelions invaded had been the night I burned a place near their home. It was the beach I visited. I left immediately and thankfully arrived at Vakfored in time."

She grabbed the journal with both hands. "There has to be more. Tell me why you attacked them."

"Because they came out and attacked me. They tried to protect their home. I defended myself, only chasing them back enough so I could fly away."

"Why did you land near the city of Skelij?"

He closed his eyes. "I should have scouted more that night. Then the War of Beasts would have never happened. I'm sorry."

She bit her lip to prevent yelling at the beast. He had apologized, but years too late because he chose to do nothing–and still did nothing. He stopped defending the city after another country tried to invade all because of him. Yelling at him would be the same as burning the book in her hand, destroying history. School taught her Vakfored's side, for they were the victors. Only Vakandi Foreldri alone could tell his side.

"Tell me about the war."

15. THE SPELL BOOK

Since the werelion attack, Vakfored attracted adventures in plenty. It became a simple for anyone to advertise their need by putting a magical sign in the air or type it up on some paper and post it on a wall. Within a day, some adventurer would grab it and go out to complete it. It gave Vakfored more time to learn how to defend itself. First, they had to finish their recent camouflage art contest and digging some reservoirs to deal with a drought that happened a few years ago. The adventurers, with time, pushed back the monsters around the city and even within parts of the Black Forest itself. Not all adventurers were successful hunters, but foolish ones who wandered into the Black Forest ill prepared.

The undead in the Black Forest grew exponentially. The adventurers did not wish to partake in Vakfored's dead burning, saying it disrespected their traditions. This led to the creation of a new type of requests, to kill the undead. Vakandi sensed the rise of a lich in the forest, watching its magic gather. Soul after soul, and not all of them were adventurers from outside of Vakfored. He wanted to step in and smite the lich before it grew any stronger. Its power had not reached that of an avalanche yet. Not that Vakfored could stop an avalanche without Vakandi's help.

He sighed, looking down at the city in the early afternoon. The Vakfored were still not solving their own problems. They were requesting others to fix everything. The city had no wall or dams protecting them after multiple generations. Others built ziggurats in that time - the lich had undead workers starting on one. The lich was a minor threat compared to others. Some adventures came to his cave trying to steal the Golden Essence's gold. Which is how Vakandi learned the difference between the confident, the unprepared, and the naïve adventurers. The naïve ones came in without knowing there was a dragon in the *very* large cave of the mountain. With a few more adventurers, and at the advice of Vakandi, the Golden Essence paid for a sign stating "Beware of Dragon". They painted the sign with a fine bright glowing yellow paint that anyone could read miles away sitting at a foothill of the mountain. It deterred a good two-thirds of the adventurers which arrived in the city.

The other third, the unprepared and the confident, were similar. The unprepared went in trembling upon visiting him. A lot of times, he sent them home with some soup and a cup of tea. They only had to pay a small fee to prevent being eaten. The confident group needed more... nibbling to be convinced to pay the handsome fee to leave empty-handed. Vakandi's gold mounted faster than when he hunted the small beasts off the mountain. It was more gold than he ever needed, and he had become unsure what to use it for.

The scary tales from the failed dragon slayers did little in deterring adventures. It only circled more "confident" adventures to come back - thankfully with more gold - and an adventurer type Vakandi had hoped to never see.

The banner of the scaly, clawed sea monster approached the city. Not a small group either, at least twenty people armed to the teeth with weapons, or at least their fingers with magic. Vakandi grumbled from his perch, looking down at the familiar banner, hiding further in the cave until they arrived. It was up to the city to decide if they wanted to welcome the sea folk. He never told the Vakfored what happened out on the coast many years ago. It had been so long that they had added three more rings to the city since. Those under the banner could be visiting peacefully, like other merchants who came through the Black Forest. Which it would then be fine if he went down to the city and introduced himself, checking in on these guests who marched in as a small squadron. No harm would happen if they did nothing. He was only going for a city visit. It had been a while since he was last there. He should go south, and definitely southeast, to confirm the monsters had thinned out along the river.

He flew around in the afternoon sun, feeling the fall chill on his wings. Winter was coming soon, already it threatened with frost to force the crops to be collected and stored away. The winter wheat glistened like the roof of the Golden Essence. The city bell rung as he approached, but it was the only noise heard. A few screams even happened as he flew over the city. Hopefully, they were the new adventurers or tourists, not the Vakfored. He cleared his throat, but ended up coughing and having to hold back a few hiccups of fire as he landed into the central ring.

This place used to be the busiest intersection, and commonly he would have to wait only a moment for the people to clear the raised podium. This time, it was desolate. The people boarded up the tall buildings nearby. Most of the broken windows from the night of the werelions covered with wood planks or shabby cloth. A few people peeked out from behind ragged curtains of the broken glass panes. He waited and finally, a group of armed personnel arrived.

The banner of the sea monster troop marched toward the podium. Their swords, staffs, spears, and hammers out ready, pointing at him. A few of the Vakfored ran over, blocking their path.

"Put your weapons away. You'll not harm our Shadow of our Sun."

The group did not react until another group of Vakfored approached them.

"Leave the dragon alone." It was a lecture to a child, not to grown armed adults, about how to behave.

The visitors lowered their weapons. All the satisfied Vakfored re-

turned to their daily lives. Not one Vakfored came up to Vakandi. The sea banner approached instead, still armed with their magic, the static charge in the air ready to snap at a command. Vakandi drew up a shield encasing the buildings in the central ring. He spread it out too much. The thin magical layer would at least be enough to protect the people from a minor spat with the sea people. The leader of the visitors noticed the action and stomped toward Vakandi with his four claw lines engraved armor. As tiny as the human was, the bricks on the podium trembled beneath his steps. Vakandi did not feel any fear.

"Dragon! Your tyranny ends. We shall free the people of Vakfored of your wrath."

A pig would have made a politer snort than what Vakandi emitted.

"Wrath? Is that what you think this is?" He moved his foot around. Realizing the current location was not a good representation of the glory of and success of Vakfored. This area needed his gold to be fixed up fast. "This is from the recent... err... past attack from a pride of werelions."

"Werelions don't perform with fire."

"I'm surprised a man of the sea is a fan of cats."

The man drew his sword and ran forward, his crew joining him. They let out a battle roar. A barbarian entered a raging mode to become stronger. All of it stopped as a bright flashing light appeared before them. Even Vakandi saw spots in his eyes for a few minutes, causing him to take flight as a precaution. He did not go too far because he remained tethered to his shield on the nearby buildings.

"The city of Vakfored has never had internal fighting - and I will uphold that tradition." A strong voice spoke, their words carried in the air.

Vakandi's eyes recovered from the flash spell and seeing the dwarf King Kirrad standing there surprised him. Bands of gold clasped his blonde, braided beard. His golden crown decorated with emeralds. Typically, the person had been soft-spoken. Here, he bellowed out a command worthy of a general. His voice reminding Vakandi of Bedruk yelling about his kilns.

Gently, Vakandi landed and tilted his head in acknowledgement to the King. People gathered around him. A variety of the representatives of the various factions of the city. The colors of agriculture, magic, the various arts, and diverse labor guilds grouped on the opposite side of the Skelij. Not one sword, spear, bow, or staff among the gathered Vakfored. King Kirrad crossed his arms. "Vakandi Foreldri, these people here are guests of Vakfored from Skelij. They," he turned to face the seaman directly, "will not be harming our Shadow of our Sun."

The seaman's jaw dropped open wide enough for a drake to slither in and call home. "The dragon listens to you?"

"In short, we give each other advice." King Kirrad smiled big through his beard, proud to be the only city with a dragon.

"The Vakfored does not always heed to it." Vakandi poked at his city. A few citizens grumbled under their breath.

"Then educate me." The Skelij leader swung his sword around. "Why does the dragon have piles of gold, but leaves your city in a state like this? A place full of decrepit buildings, waiting for crime to happen."

"Intruders should hold their tongues," hissed Vakandi.

The sword swung around and pointed back at a scaly foot. Vakandi wanted this man to start it, so he could take a bite and end this argument. King Kirrad stormed over, heels clicking, and kicked the sword away. "Leave at once for your digressions."

The squad of the Skelij charged at aggression to their leader. They did not even hesitate to free their weapons. The spells of earlier launched up into the air, hitting Vakandi with water, ice, and wind spells. They knew his weakness. He personally told it their ancestors years ago on the beach. Each hit that landed on his scales caused him to grunt and regret his past words. He put a claw between King Kirrad and the attackers. Smoke billowed out of his mouth as weapons hit his foot. A few pierced through, bits of blood dripped out. He could handle a few hits and get to his elixir, the Vakfored matter more. He blew fire at the squadron, trying

to keep the King safe.

Except the Skelij leader was still near King Kirrad. He grabbed the weaker dwarf's arm, bent it and made a shield of the King. "Tell the flying lizard to back off!"

The troops screamed and tried to reorganize a new defensive line closer to the buildings with the magic shield Vakandi made. A cowardice effective plan. The shield would not withstand his fire. The heated anger slid from Vakandi's mouth. "Let him go."

"Vakandi. Please listen." King Kirrad panicked and still not one Vakfored nearby drew a weapon. Centuries of helping the city grow, and they could not defend themselves. No matter what weapon or monster walked in, no defensive guards stood up to stop them.

Vakandi raised his head and pulled his fire magic in, and left the shields out. "Release the King and leave."

"You'll just eat us the moment I let him go. He comes with me." The Skelij pulled a dagger out and pushed it next to King Kirrad's throat. "Let's go. Carefully, down the road."

Vakandi Foreldri growled at being challenged back. This city was his and his people literally had let another threat step in and threaten him. The city needed a kick in the buttocks to learn how to clean up their own messes, like the inner ring from the night of the werelions. A full generation had aged up since the attack. They had built the outer fifteenth ring, they could have repaired the inner ring by now. The King scuttled along with the Skelij. When the knife loosened, he did not even glance back or try to break free. Not a single sign he wanted help, just acceptance of his situation of being used.

Bit by bit the magic weaved off the houses and into a small narrow pillar of a fire spell. Straight and narrow like a needle hitting right where he wanted, behind King Kirrad's footsteps. No person would defeat the great Vakandi Foreldri. Especially not even a pitiful group of twenty of them. The fire column spell launched out of his mouth and he chased down the intruders. Closing the distance quickly. The bricks of the path flew up and did not shift back to where they belonged. The people of Vakfored screamed out of the way. The Skelij hands slew a few as they tried to run for the exit of the city. Rumors of what happened to the werelions must have arrived at the Skelij's home. There would be no refuge for them inside the Vakfored homes. Only the leader remained, determined to hold on to his hostage, which slowed him down. With a flick of his claw, he sent the Skelij leader flying. Blood filled the air as King Kirrad cried out in pain from a knife attack. With two claws, Vakandi scooped up the King into the sky beneath him. He pulled the fire from his stomach and blew right behind the troop, chasing them out of the city. Less than ten made it out. Enough to send the message back to any foolish dragon-slaying adventures to never try this again, or a burnt path of death would follow them.

16. THE INTRUSION

The Burnt Road is the worst street in the city." Sisal interrupted Vakandi's tale. "It's the quickest path from the inner ring to out of the city. You would think the Guild of Transportation would do a better job maintaining it."

Vakandi Foreldri tilted his head as he flicked some spider bodies into the fire. They finished cleaning out the barracks. Sisal shut the window and confirmed the lock was in place. "I thought they paved it years ago with new bricks."

"It is, but they did not build it with the winters in mind or the heavy weighted carts that come through. They should have dug deeper and done a double paving. I hear some cities in the mountains did that and they hold up fine."

"The road less traveled on is generally not easier." He jumbled over the idiom.

"I'm not talking about accessibility. I'm talking about smoothness. Carts weave in and around the potholes all the time now. Do you think your fire damaged the road?"

"No. I paid for that path's repairs."

"With the gold you took from the adventurers."

For the first time ever, a dragon looked away from a person out of embarrassment. Sisal laughed, threw in the last of the logs into the hearth and used the chance to pocket the spell book. She grabbed a coin in her pocket and flipped it around, trying to guess heads or tails. The coin landed with the plated tail of a dragon.

"You said all this gold here belonged to the Golden Essence. What happened to all the gold you took from the adventurers?" It's not like Vakandi strolled down to market street to buy food or had to pay for his housing. He hopefully spent some of it on himself, and not just Vakfored.

"I have invested most of it. But yes, there was a decent amount gathered."

The funeral proceedings were not a small cost. "Thank you for making sure everyone has a chance to say goodbye. But why didn't you keep any of it for yourself?"

"I felt... that the death of the hundreds who died in the war were my fault. I should have killed all twenty of those people from the sea to prevent them from returning with an army."

Sisal closed her mouth. All the books talked about how the city of Vakfored buried itself after the War of Beasts. They created walls to block out the forest and mountains. They dug deeper into the earth to hide and they burned their dead before they had their last night in order to forget the past. The scar on the city from the war was darker than the black scorched-earth that was once been the Burnt Road. The War of Beasts was a fight of water versus fire. All of Vakfored knew that if they had faced the people of Skelij out by the ocean, they would have lost. The Skelij still had the power of the Paondel River on their backs to face down the great dragon. It worked as a spear that wedged into the city.

"Do you want me to tell you my side of the story of the war?" Vakandi spoke softly, as if the dragon did not want to be heard.

Sisal hugged herself to prevent the strong feeling in her gut from creating a bigger frog in her throat.

"I have to." The words croaked out.

Hearing his side of the stories made it harder to do her mission, and almost possible to forgive him. She wanted to run. Every history book talked about the War of Beasts with one opener. It took two years to build the fifteenth ring of the city. It took one hour to destroy it. She did not want to hear the tale from the dragon who burned it down. She did not want to forgive him. It was not her place to do so.

17. THE SPLIT

On the day Vakandi chased the Skelijs out, he made a promise with King Kirrad. They would not repeat the things the King said and did while being carried by a dragon claws. In exchange, King Kirrad agreed to build a gate and watchtowers. An enemy could walk around a gate if there was no wall or fence, but it was at least the start of the city doing their homework alone.

"I don't want a wall. It forces our city to be contained," King Kirrad complained. "Creativity is not something you hold back."

"You paint on a canvas and its beauty is eternal in that small rectangular shape. No one touches it, and you hang it up to protect it in a frame. Create a wall that is your frame." He did not mention how easily fire could destroy a painting in a dragon's hoard.

The King harrumphed but nodded in agreement. When the work did not begin by the afternoon because they were preparing the pyres at the Engill's Perigon, Vakandi gave them more time. He watched the city from a distance, patiently he waited and respected their rites. For the last few centuries, they honored him to light a pyre. Today, he felt wrong to intrude, and no one in the palace touched the hearth to ask him to do so. Instead, those at the funeral passed the torch along and put it into the timber the moment the sun peeked over the horizon. Fire from the earth to carry the body to the sun and air so the soul may join the cycle again. By afternoon, only a pile of ashes remained. He flew to his landing spot by the funeral to pay his respects. Silently he lowered his head there, pondering his actions which had created this situation.

Landing outside of Vakfored yesterday would have kept the people safe. Telling them about what happened years ago on the beach would have protected them. They might have built a wall by now and not needed the mercenaries to fight their battles for them.

Someone at last approached him, an orc who untied their eggplant purple hat and bowed deeply, then stood straight, looking up at Vakandi.

"I did not believe the rumors when they said there was a peaceful dragon." Their accent pinning them as an adventurer, as well as the short sword and the multiple daggers on their person. "I figured this city got what it deserved when you started burning the street. But then you saved the King. And here you are, honoring the dead from yesterday. What a peculiar dragon."

"Are you a well-equipped historian with all those weapons?" He mocked back.

They tilted their head back, the sun catching glimpses of black hair. "Oh, I don't have the drive to sit and read books all day. I prefer using my hands and brain differently."

"Then why approach me?"

The orc placed a green hand on Vakandi. "Dragons are extremely powerful rulers of a domain. This city is your domain, yet in the past few weeks of me being here, it is clear the relationship between you and the city has turned tyrannical. I was certain a job request would go up to slay you soon. But no tyrant would visit a funeral."

"Nor a wandering adventurer, unless you knew someone who died."

"I only joined because I saw you come here. The city owes you much, growing this close to the Black Forest. But tell me, why are you no longer hunting the small monsters which roam nearby?"

"It was time the Vakfored grew and met the world again."

The orc took their hand off and stretched their arms out. "It's going to take a lot of mercenaries and adventurers to keep them safe. I'm going to get rich–maybe even famous. Thanks, Shadow of the Sun." The orc put their hat back on.

"What's your name?"

"Kennezben Konst the Third."

Vakandi tilted his head. "Until we meet again. If you feel brave enough, visit my cave."

The orc lowered their head and walked away. It definitely would not be the last time they saw each other. It hurt to know that an outsider of a few weeks could see the vulnerability of the city. A single dragon could not keep hundreds of thousands of people safe. If an army showed up, divided on the East and West of the river, Vakandi would have to choose which side of the city the enemy got to destroy.

The King needed to create a work order today. He flew to the inner ring, standing proudly, waiting for King Kirrad to arrive. It did not take along for the meek ruler to approach. He rode up in a carriage to the platform and then walked to his seat, picking it up after yesterday's scuffle, and faced Vakandi.

"What brings you here today?" King Kirrad inquired. No greeting or honoring the dragon. A flush broke out over the man's face and he broke eye contact for a moment. Likely recalling how he had bawled in Vakandi's claw more than when a knife was at his throat.

"I see no watchtower work has begun."

"We were grieving our dead -"

"I gave you a full day and through the morning, as is proper. I demand it to be done now." Vakandi had coddled the city enough. It was time for a stern approach.

"We need to survey the area thoroughly, design the buildings, gather resources, and hire a guard to notify you. These things take time."

Vakandi's tail swung about in annoyance. "Do not notify me with the guard! They are to alert an army or a defense that a threat is coming so you can prepare."

"But then, what would you do all day? Lounge about in your gold?"

"Yes. I would like to retire from raising Vakfored after centuries."

"What do we gain out of this situation that you are forcing upon us?"

"Knowing you could survive any situation, that you can stand on your own. Instead, you pay these mercenaries to do the work for you."

King Kirrad stood up done with the pleasantry talk. "They do what they are best at, just like the city of Vakfored does what we are best at. You should do the same."

"Why are you not getting it into your head? The city is stagnant, it is no longer growing."

"Our words are apparently going in and out of your ears, too. We are growing, we are a desired city of the arts and crafts. You used to appreciate our non-aggressive approach to other lands - and beasts. Apparently, the way we have lived for centuries is not up to the great dragon's vision."

The fire burned in Vakandi's mouth for being talked down to by a mortal. He counted to three to organize his thoughts and bring back the point of this meeting. "What if I'm not around anymore? What if the werelions come in again? Who will save you?"

"That's why we have the adventurers. And before you mention the kingdom of Skelij, I'm already sending a diplomat over to clear up this mess. They are friends and welcome here. As the Shadow of our Sun, I had expected you to keep your temper better. As we agreed, I will build the watchtowers in an appropriate amount of time. Have a good evening."

The King walked down the platform and got in his carriage, no longer appearing to be the weak person, but a confident leader. Vakandi flew off to survey his domain, and clean up any mess the mercenaries missed. It was the only way he knew how to get rid of the frustration that boiled in his chest. A bit of fresh seared meat to chew on always lightened his mood. He flew away from the northern mountains to the more delectable gamey meat in the south, away from the Black Forest.

Only one group of adventurers shouted up to him this time, and it was to say hello. They were slowly getting used to the thought of a peaceful dragon within the city. One of the largest species in existence, and he comforted the people. A smile stretched across his face as he spat out fire to get a free ranging bison. He quite enjoyed being loved by the people of Vakfored.

As he chewed on the bison, he realized the language lately had not been of love, but annoyance from his hatchlings. They disrespected his vast knowledge, saying they knew more. He had centuries of knowledge on them. He saw cities rise, and multiple fall. Vakfored had outlived most of them, only by his grace. Even an outside mercenary could see the wedge growing between Vakandi and the Vakfored.

A chill grew in the evening light as winter crept closer. The currents of the ocean carried icy winds into the valley. The first snowfall could be on any day. The comfort of winter of being stuck inside by a burning hearth became a false hope.

Off on the shores, outside of the eyes of Vakandi Foreldri, shields were gathering to make a defense to withstand the blast of a dragon's fire breath. Scale by scale, they built a defense over the course of a few days. While the King Kirrad and the people of Vakfored bickered on where to put the watchtowers and how to design them.

The desire of the Skelij drove them to achieve their goal. The hatred of doing a forced task caused the Vakfored to procrastinate.

It cost them the fifteenth ring of the city.

18. THE ARMY

The afternoon of the next day melted the night frost away. A few bison, and one fish sat in the bottom of his stomach. Vakandi rarely gorged so much that it left him grounded and unable to fly. Last night he did and had to sleep outside on the plains. He was undisturbed the whole night and woke up shivering in the cold, but it calmed the heat that raged inside him. It took him a bit to feel warm and get moving again. Winters always made him sluggish.

The city finally began building one watchtower on the side he currently slept on. They should have had that tower decades ago… but at least it was a start. Stretching out his wings, he called forth the fire magic within and warmed his bones and scales. With a powerful push, he flew up into the air to see the land in a different light. King Kirrad had made some fair points. The people of Vakfored were not fighters or conquerors. Enticing mercenaries could work as a solution, just needed a constant high count of them. If the city ever drew the ire or jealously of another nation, it would be impossible to hire enough mercenaries in time to save the city. They still needed a wall to protect themselves. They would still need Vakandi.

If they built the wall, he could reward them by paying them to paint

the wall full of murals. As he flew higher in the air, he glanced toward the ocean in the southwest, unease in his gut. He should have scouted toward the ocean last night. Better now than later. While flying, he traced the path from the newly named Burnt Road out of the city along the Paondel River. From there, the path entered the valley and became a less traveled minor road. King Kirrad created a few work orders to help smooth this path, but the focus of the project did not reach the ocean. Merchants rarely came from this side of the Black Forest.

By twilight, he reached the shores of the coast, but stopped and hovered in the air before coming too close. Lanterns sat on the boats along the shore, lighting up multiple sails. The Skelij had created a large campsite stretching across the coast and into the land. An entire army had taken camp under the symbol of a scaly, clawed monster.

He flew closer and cries erupted nearby. A flare exploded in the dark sky. It glowed right above a quickly assembled watchtower. They threw it together with the boat masts and one of the jib sails to act as a nest. The pitiful structure served its job as the alerted army gathered to go face the threat. Vakandi resisted roaring or doing anything aggressive. In fact, he backed up. These were typical non-Vakfored people acting scared of a dragon. He had to take the peaceful option. King Kirrad declared he sent a diplomat.

"Where is the Vakfored citizen?" He questioned.

Like with his hatchlings, he learned to count to ten as the people tried to gather a response. They simply translated their reply into an ice attack raging at him. He flew wide, but it clipped his tail. He rained fire down at the base of the encampment. As predicted, he needed to stay far out of range from the multiple snowballs, icicles, and freezing rain attacks. The air out here by the ocean was heavy with cold and water magic. The people of Skelij were wise to come after him near winter, but before the storms of the ocean.

The best thing he could do in this situation would be to force them away from the ocean. This was not a spot for him to fight. He took flight, the bitter bite of their ice attacks nipping at his scales. Enough to leave an itch. He should have spawned a shield the moment he noticed the army. Calling the wind, he raced back to Vakfored and landed on the inner ring in the middle of the night.

He roared out and shot up fire straight into the air. The city needed to prepare immediately. This was not the time to sleep. If the army of Skelij marched to them now, they would arrive in two days' time. With it being the middle of the night, the artists who stayed up till dawn were the ones who got to him first. A few had color dye or ink on them. Stains covered one bowl, too soft and not hardened by flames. Times were going to change, and it would be guards who would greet him in the future.

"There is an army by the shores. They belong to the very people who were here earlier." He spoke loudly and slowly so everyone would hear without an echo.

The carriage of King Kirrad finally arrived. "I told you to stay out of it. I sent a diplomat."

"They are dead. I asked for your diplomat and the army attacked me."

"Maybe a person would have been more accepted. Your presence is a bit terrifying to those on the outside."

"I didn't take kindly to them shooting me in your own city, which they mocked."

King Kirrad kept a stoic face, not saying one word. A large purple hat with a feather sticking out approached the podium. Once removed, the grin of Kennezben Konst the Third beamed up to the dragon. "Seems to me, us adventurers and mercenaries are going to have a big request coming in. Who's going to fund the gold for this protection against an army?"

For an orc, they were accurate and right on the short, stubby nose. Like their sharp teeth, their weapons were out for display and ready to face any threat head on, even if outnumbered.

Vakandi had hope in this person. "I shall supply the gold if they protect the city."

"Ah yes, but how do I know you have the funds? Rumor has it you and the Golden Essence are in cahoots, and I've heard how empty the vaults are at the bank."

"I am a dragon. I have a hoard."

The orc fluffed the feather on their hat. "I'll write up a contract and gather the fighters."

Their words gave a bit of relief. Vakandi had to start the next plan. He twisted his neck to look at King Kirrad. "They'll be coming in through the low end of the valley to here. Some will take the river, but most will be by land." He did not expand why. "We need a barricade built now to slow them down. Those on the river will be sitting ducks for some basic mage spells. The Skelij appears to be specialized in ice and water. I will teach you how to use the earth and fire to counter properly."

"Will we have enough time? Shouldn't we retreat to your cave?" The King had to be thinking about the newly built guest room in the first cavern. It could only house twenty people. The rest of the families would need to take refuge in the main cavern of the mountain.

"I can't fit an entire city into my cave and it be a matter of time until the army climbed up there after destroying Vakfored. Build the barricades as I have ordered. The mages know how to turn earth into statues and art. They can make a simple defense. Others know how to make high heat to glaze their potter work. They can throw a simple fireball."

Kennezben raised a hand. "If I may, we can defend only part of the city. We won't be able to defend the river from the bridge alone."

"I need the fighters available to move quickly depending on where the army appears," Vakandi replied. "I'll take care of the river."

"Unlike you, we don't have wings to dart from one side of the city or another. If you give a half a day's heads up on where this army is, we can station ourselves - but the lack of a wall will leave us very vulnerable."

King Kirrad waved a hand in the air. "You're an outsider who doesn't understand our culture."

"No, but I like it here. Let's keep this city alive another day. At a payment, of course. Even the arts cost money."

No one said anything to disagree. Vakandi already made the agreement to fund the defense. That was enough for Kennezben. They left for the night to figure out what needed to be gathered and completed come first light.

Vakandi did not sleep, instead he circled around the city, seeing every vulnerability. They left themselves completely exposed on the Black Forest side during the battle. Any monster, like the lich, could finally come in. The people were taking this too casually. An army of ten thousand strong would soon storm down on the city, and only a few hundred adventurers and mercenaries were available to protect it. Even if all the mages in the city learned to do basic defense magic, they would still be out powered. They needed to slow the army down and force them to funnel in. The Skelij could not climb over the mountains since they were coming from the ocean. If he could prevent them from crossing the river with their boats, they could limit the side of the city being attacked to just the East.

The Skelij already knew that Vakandi had discovered their position. Delaying departure would be foolish. They would rush toward the exposed city immediately. Vakandi expedited his plans to hinder the enemy. He needed to do two plans, but both mattered on where his enemy was. He raced down the Paondel River, the moon's reflection dancing on its surface as it popped out of the clouds. Normally a tranquil sight, but now he wanted the clouds to move to help hide him. He stayed low, just above the treetops, in case the enemy already moved and hid in the forest like the moon now did in the clouds.

No fish jumped out of the waters tonight, but neither did a boat or signs of the army. As he got close to the ocean, he veered course to go further southwest, just as a crack of gray greeted into the world. He had to hurry before they saw him and fought back. He had not raced along the lands over this side of the river in centuries. A sightseeing visit could hap-

pen later. If there had been more time, he would fly further out into the ocean and come directly behind the entire army. Time was too limited as the sun threated to expose him. He weaved a magical shield around him.

He veered directions and flew out over the ocean, just along the coast, curving to come around the side of the Skelij's ships. They had dismantled a few of their boats, with a few smaller docking boats already sitting near the river. With one fireball, he shot at the smaller boats first. Then the next few attacks were quick shots, making sure the fire would spread enough to destroy the other boats near them. By the time he finished that, the red sun peaked over the horizon and down on the enraged. With haste, he flew to attack the next collection of ships along the shore near the river. With a force from his wings, he generated a gale to push the boats into the bay of the river next to their smoldering brethren. Smoke rose from the initial burns. He flew over to another set and released a torrent of fire. The heat of his blaze turned into steam as a fountain of water rose to meet him. He took the chilly ocean water hit, and it rippled around his magic shield, but as the water geyser continued, spider web like fractures formed.

He had to stop his attack and flew away into the smoke from the ships and along the water's edge. Any time he saw a boat, he blew another fireball. The first two hit, but after more water rose to block his attacks, more ships were being saved and his shield weakened. Flying high into the sunrise, above the smoke, he sensed the being from decades past. Something that he could expose if he attacked it with a powerful gust to part the waters. Using such an attack would give away his position to the ocean monster and an entire army.

It did not matter as the creature broke the water's surface, challenging Vakandi. It was larger than the palace in Vakfored, even when half submerged. Its outer shell shrugged off a fireball attack without the use of a magical shield. The tightly knit scales gave even the eyes protection as he opened its jaw to gargle up at the dragon. A skeljaskrimsli. The sharp teeth were the skeljaskrimsli's weakest ability. Their claws were stronger and longer, strong enough to cut through a dragon's skin. Its ice and water magic were a complete counter to a fire dragon. The cold gathered around the beast and shards of ice grew to match the size of its teeth, then it launched out the ice at its flying advisory.

He wrapped his wings around him and departed back to the path he came, before spreading his wings out to rise back above the trees on land. Icicles the size of pins and needles attacked his shield before a large glacial attack shattered it and slammed into him. Out of control from the impact, he crashed into the ground. Trees splintered with his force, a bone in his wing fractured in response as the foliage and dirt flew up into his face. At least he remained upright, though the one wing absorbed too much of the force of when he crashed. He could not quickly fly home to warn the Vakfored. For the first time since he was a hatchling, he took off running on the ground, grimacing as his wing bounced into trees.

The forest had always been alive with sounds, even at night, but now not even the night birds and insects chirped as the change in cold magic grew close. The thick forest slowed him down, but he would not let it trap him. He forced through it, carving an alternative path, embracing each new bruise and cut as nature fought back. This pain was normal when the war was beginning.

This current pace or pushing through the woods would be too slow, and would only get slower when he got near the Black Forest. The skeljaskrimsli could crawl down the river and destroy Vakfored before Vakandi could get there. He grimaced and called on the wind, even as the chill engulfed it and frost encroached on him. He wanted to burn the surrounding woods to chase the frigid air back. All of his magic and efforts needed to be conserved, and he had to get home. He pushed up into the air with his good wing, and the icy wind carried the other wing. Daring a glance back, in the light of a half of the burning ship, he saw the outline of the skeljaskrimsli encroaching toward him along the coast. Vakandi focused on getting away before any other magical attacks came after him.

19. THE SNOW

Previously, the flight to the ocean took less than half a day. Without both of Vakandi's wings, it took until late in the evening. A full day lost with him lumbering through and above the forest. Keeping himself in the air was difficult and required him to land from time to time to regain his strength. As he got closer to the city of Vakfored, he stared out in the southeast direction along the river. He feared of ice floating down the current and of the skeljaskrimsli swimming up and devouring everyone.

The image weighed heavily on him and he landed harder than normal on the podium. The red and white bricks clattered and cracked, but still tried to shift back to their normal position. For years the Vakfored abandoned the central ring. Today it bustled with activity. The people scattered out of his way, but stayed nearby. Magical boards were up, listing the supplies and the unique skill sets the mages of the city had. King Kirrad, with a colorful quill dripping with deep blue ink, wrote in the air, listening to the congregated council. "Well, this meeting has been interrupted. We'll continue later."

"His wing!" Voiced Kennezben. Their large purple hat complimenting the red shirt they wore by the center of the boards.

They ran over to Vakandi's crooked wing. He lowered it carefully to them. It easily stayed spread out with how swollen it became. It became a habit to let the city inspect an injury after all the avalanches and monster attacks. "Mx. Konst, don't tell me you are also a healer. It seems against your nature."

"Says the dragon, protecting a city of people." They retorted and pulled out a glass flask filled with a shimmering liquid. An elixir of life that most other dragons would be envious of. "Will this help?"

"It would. But those are extremely valuable. Are you sure?"

The orc took off their hat and waved it around at the people nearby. "Shadow of my Sun, given the choice between the people, the King himself, or you right before a battle, I would always pick the big, friendly dragon in front of me."

"And I am assuming it means you are picking me even over yourself?"

"I'm taking care of my coin purse and writing it up as part of the expense report I'll give you once this battle is over."

"That's very professional of you." He pointed a claw to where a human and orc carried a barrel with a golden painted dragon on it. "But I have my own serving size and concentration. Thank you." He said to the orc. Knowing they ran on gold in their pocket would make completing all requests easier. Especially compared to those nearby who waited until they were in the mood to complete a chore.

One claw punctured the top of the barrel, tilted it back and swallowed the shimmering red liquid. It had a taste of two gold piles. The potion helped to decrease the swelling drastically, creating an itching relieving sensation as the wing repaired. He thanked those who brought the barrel before returning to the task at hand. Then he continued his conversation with Kennezben. "Did the Vakfored tell you about their own healing potions?"

"The ones that delay death by greeting it halfway? Yes. Let me get more for you."

"That won't be necessary." King Kirrad walked over. "Our healing magics do not work on Vakandi Foreldri."

"He's correct." Vakandi did not want to give sensitive details to the adventurer who took on monster slaying quests. It was a very thin line between monster and the guardian dragon of Vakfored. King Kirrad avoided an explanation too.

Vakandi pointed to the King. "You'll all be needing them, and distribute them to areas in the southeast immediately. As well as near the river."

"These hypothetical positions I'm assuming deal with why you look disheveled," King Kirrad probed.

The adventurer cleared his throat. It turns out they had some respect for the King's position after all. Kennezben bit his lip to prevent saying anything about how a mortal should not insult the looks of a dragon, no matter how factual they were. The elixir healed him. It did not wash off the leaves and dirt that covered him. Vakandi tapped one of his fore claws on the podium to a slow beat as he counted to ten before replying in an educational matter. "The army had boats. I wanted to burn them down to prevent them from riding on them straight into the middle of the city. To slow their movement down the river by forcing them to walk."

"And making them desperate to succeed because they can't go back home now." King Kirrad barked. "You should've confided with me instead of making a mess again."

"So, we could decide on what color flags we should use? I am betting you debated on which color ink displayed the best. Deciding which way to display the barricades so it still didn't impede the merchants - but somehow slowed the army down. You know nothing about war compared to my centuries of knowledge. You don't even know they have a skeljaskrimsli. It's going to swim down Paondel River. Freeze it and the entire city while the Skelij raid and destroy everything."

King Kirrad's face reddened. He pointed the sharp glistened blue ink tip at Vakandi. "You don't know... You never listen. Mythical beasts are nothing to us." He turned and faced everyone. A glance at Kennezben

showed the orc had paled. King Kirrad shouted to the crowd. "We will not give up just because they now have a water monster on their side. We've faced various emissaries before. Like a knot in the wood, we are determined to straighten it out and show off its beauty. We'll use our stubbornness to win this thing. Now focus."

King Kirrad marched back to the boards, determined to save his people his way. Vakandi huffed, understanding how little people of Vakfored would listen to him now. At the face of a threat, they should have united, not be at the opposite ends during their biggest turmoil moment. They were the same as the oil paintings in his cave dripping onto the floor. Once structured and beautiful, but under fire, they were a mess. It saddened him to see that his snoring had destroyed their beautiful works. He hid the mess behind piles of gold coins, but what came for Vakfored, no amount of gold could hide them.

At least the pile of gold would act as a wall with the mercenaries, but only in one spot. His eyes wandered to the border of the city where the fifteenth ring sat with its spread-out buildings. It took the longest to build once they started it, two full years to gather the supplies. Three bridges crossed the river, simple things a monster in the river could destroy. The tall houses and office and buildings offset by the various workshops. They created all the rings peacefully thanks to Vakandi hunting and removing the monsters. The next ring might not be so lucky and mark the city with a raised bump sticking out where a gate would sit along the future wall. Like the shape of his dragon scale, all because of the battle to come. Forcing Vakfored to become resilient like a dragon trapped inside.

"See anything?" Kennezben stood by him as the rest of the people retreated to act out the plans King Kirrad had. The King's carriage rode down the road to the palace.

"Nothing but vulnerabilities."

"I don't know about that. I apologize if I am overstepping, but I get where you are coming from. You and I have the way of war and fighting in our blood. It's not in the people of Vakfored. But they have ideas - they have tools to use as weapons that most cities would not even consider because of how rare the tool is. For example, they have a decent number of fireworks and know how to trigger them by having them stepped on. They have an endless amount of paint to help hide the doors of the houses out there. Already they are painting to cover them and sealing them up as best as possible. Traps are even being set with all the oil and fat in town from the best kitchens and pastry chefs. These things aren't what a typical army plans for."

Vakandi frowned, all that paint ruined because of this battle. He would make the Skelij pay for this - after he destroyed their guardian. The fire ignited in his belly, ready to burn that beast. He stretched both his wings out, the pain and swelling from earlier finally gone.

"Thank you for your words of encouragement. I shall work hard like my people. I'm going to fix that river."

"Hmmm. You have some impressive dwarves here. Don't touch the river. Let me talk to King Kirrad and the dwarves for you."

"I can talk to them."

"You two have done nothing but fight. Let me be a mediator. Someone who understands where you are coming from, and someone who has been learning from the people what being Vakfored means."

Vakandi felt it would be impossible for an outsider to understand, but here they were in the middle of preparations for a battle. They only stayed around to line their pockets. He wanted to know if the mercenary could actually listen. "Tell me, what does it mean?"

"In the circle of our lives, nothing binds you, even death."

"Mx. Konst the Third, I'll trust the river to you. Make it shallow - no. I will trust you to work with the city. Just make sure it will weaken the skeljaskrimsli. Also, have the people on the southeast and east side ready to retreat out of their homes. Give up that fifteenth ring."

"You're asking them to give up their homes? That's the toughest hardtack anyone will ever have to swallow. They're already setting up the traps. Trust them."

Vakandi did not want to ruin another relationship. It had been a while since any of the people had even wanted to talk to him. A millennium ago, he desired the silence of his cave. These days it felt lonely. He would find the peace between him and his people once this battle was over. He would make sure his Vakfored were safe. Flying high above the city with his repaired wing, he circled the city clockwise. As he followed its curvature, he saw the streets between each ring of the city, the roads that welcomed anyone in. The city made them a perfect bull's-eye marker for any enemy.

"I will keep you safe."

He returned to the valley where he rested the other day. Flying over the farm fields, the wheat was being collected on this side of the city. This would likely be the last chance he could get to sleep for a while. Even with the elixirs, he needed to recover his mental strength. Out here he could remain at watch and wake to the slightest rumbling of any army approaching.

It was not a restful sleep, but multiple mini-naps. Every breaking stick had him jolting awake. A better rest would have been in his cave, especially since nothing happened all night. He knew nothing would. Even when injured, he flew faster than humans could walk from the ocean to here. They would have been licking their wounds and figuring out a new plan.

White, large snowflakes slowly drifted down and the air temperature dropped. The first snowfall came earlier than ever before. He closed his eyes and reached for the magics. Normally cold magic evaded him. Now it danced next to him. Though winter was coming naturally, magic forced it forward faster.

The Skelijs did not lick their wounds like a hurt feline. They charged forward under the guidance of the skeljaskrimsli. Vakandi could not smell them as the snowfall increased in the plains he stood on. This weather favored the seamen who trained in it. They were battle borne. A dragon's attack at their encampment and the snow did now slow them. They would glide across the frost with weapons ready.

20. THE WALL

Vakandi took to the air and headed southeast along the river, looking for the army. It did not take long for him to hear them. He tried flying high enough to avoid getting caught by the skeljaskrimsli. This high in the snow clouds made it impossible to see the enemy in the temperate forest near the plains and the cold caused an ache in his muscles. He did not hear the beast lumbering through the woods destroying it. It was not giving up the advantages of being in the river. If he wanted to spot the enemy's exact location, he would have to fly lower.

He swerved back around, calling upon a magical shield to surround him, and returned in the direction he knew was home. Today, all other magical shields were for the Vakfored. His Vakfored would not fall, no matter what.

He roared out to wake everyone. The windows and doors rattling from the volume. It had to be early morning, but because of the dark overcast, it was hard to discern. Darkness would not destroy Vakfored today. His flame would light the day and see them through.

"The Skelij army is hours out. Ready yourselves!"

He circled around the city, watching the umber clay shingles turn to white. The murals on the city repelled the snow and stood out with their vibrant colors. The same oil paint covered the doors and windows of the fifteenth ring. It exposed all the access points into the homes of the Vakfored. The snow did not stick to the paint no matter how three-dimensional the art looked. The ledge and rough stone were only painted to look that way. It did not catch the snow.

Vakandi hovered above the ground, in fear of setting off any hidden traps on the outer ring. He noticed the lack of footprints in the snow by the buildings. He knew it meant none of the people had not moved yet. "People of the fifteenth ring! Retreat now!" He roared again. A few people got out, but no one took anything with them. A dwarf still in her nightcap pointed up at Vakandi and shook her head as she talked with her neighbor, a human with a scarf wrapped around their neck.

"Get to safety." He growled, annoyed at their dilly dallying around.

Kennezben's purple hat stood out more than the artistically painted doors as they approached Vakandi on horseback. "Shadow of my Sun, is this the way they'll be coming?"

"Yes. In the river swims the skeljaskrimsli. It has more icicles in its mouth than teeth now." He remembered the fight the day before, how it had formed the threatening attack.

The orc mumbled a curse under their breath. "The miners worked hard. It's eighty percent ready."

"How much longer until it's completed?"

They shook their head, the snow that gathered on the hat's brim fell off. "I gave the order to say that they need to evacuate and that they pull the lever on my signal."

"And how will you know?"

They glared up, eyes narrowing. "I'm experienced in fights. I know when to drain the river to weaken the skeljaskrimsli. When I do, you burn the beast."

"Where is this drain in the river?"

"A cannon's shot from the fifteenth ring, the shallow spot where the forest touches the river. It was the furthest we could build it. Don't delay any attacks. The reservoirs won't hold the entire river."

The houses by the road had multiple barricades set up in front of the path, forcing groups of people to weave in and out or split up. "Are the archers in place?" Vakandi asked.

"I'll get everyone set up. King Kirrad is getting the children and older folks to safety in your cave. I... I'll nudge those at this ring and the next to retreat." Vakandi wanted to grab the roofs of the houses and yell at the people to get out. To make them move faster. Every time he spoke lately, they had openly defied him back. "Thank you."

"The oil pit traps, they are a hundred meters out from this. You know as well as I do the skeljaskrimsli is causing the drop in temperature so it would snow. Leave those pits for our archers."

"I don't need oil to make anything burn."

"Then cook us some skeljaskrimsli, Shadow of my Sun," jested Kennezben.

"I hope we meet again."

"Oh, we will. You have a big invoice to pay when this is done."

They rode off on their horse, and the snow fell in wet, disgusting cold globs now. Vakandi flew just above the tree line, listening and searching for his prey. His shield absorbing the snow for him as he flew away from the river. The goal would be to force the enemy to funnel over the traps and to the main road. Slowing them down to be easy pickings for the mercenaries while he battled their beast.

The enemy did not carry torches or use magic to guide by. The lights from Vakfored were a beacon reflecting off all the snow, guiding them through the unknown terrain. They were prepared for fighting in the snow, but not for fighting a flying dragon. He scouted these woods for a millennium for monsters. He knew the ancestors of the trees and the creatures that lived here. Spotting an army hiding in the woods was an effortless task for him soaring this low. Once upon them, he let out all his rage from the past few days. The fire burned with his frustration from his failed attempts to prepare the Vakfored, from protecting them, from not understanding them. He was a dragon with no similarities with the Vakfored.

But it did not stop him from protecting his hatchlings.

The screams of the Skelij guided him as he burned through them. Magical shields stood up to save a few, but not all. He picked up a handful and threw them in the direction they came from. How he wished he could launch them back into the ocean. A few arrows bounced off his own magical shield, and he laughed.

"Little prey better run."

People are intelligent creatures compared to the typical beasts he hunted. But they were still slow and could be predictable when in clustered groups like this. A few confident soldiers hunted him this far from their river. The rest, the unprepared and naïve soldiers, turned to run toward their own protector, the one who could stop the dragon. Vakandi burned all he could and threw them into a pile to become a pyre for his wrath.

Satisfied that this group ran to the main road, he flew back toward Vakfored. The rearguard of the Skelij was still safe. He wanted the enemy to die or have a clear path back to where they came–even if they did not have boats. A dragon should have a hard outer shell to protect themself and their heart, like the shields the enemy wore. Helping the city of Vakfored grow made him soft to give these people a chance to run away. All because he wanted to stop the biggest threat from hurting his people.

As he hovered over the main road into the city, people loitered and talked with the mercenaries on Burnt Road. Some saw his approach and meandered back inside to their homes of the fifteenth ring. A tall orc with their black hair buried by the snow approached Vakandi. He almost didn't recognize them without the hat.

"How far out are they? A few seers reported seeing smoke." Kennezben wasted no time on asking additional questions, straight to the point like the scimitar in their hand. A trained mercenary.

"Less than two hours. Why are people still in their homes? They need to evacuate."

The orc grimaced. "They believe in you and everything they've done to save the place. Scout out the river and confirm the Skelij aren't on the other side."

"I was already going to."

Wind and now snow beneath his wings, he charged toward the southern side of the Paondel River. He strengthened his shield once more, in case a surprise attack happened from the skeljaskrimsli hiding in the water depths. To face a powerful creature would be a challenge, but this was now his domain, his nest, his city, his people. They would not destroy his hatchlings.

His blood pressure increased once he arrived at the river. Large floating chunks of ice gathered by the first bridge for the fifteenth ring. Following the flow, not even an hour's walk down the river, an ice dam neared completion. Soldiers sat at the ready while the mages built them a land bridge to cross. Vakfored breathed down on them with the rage to melt their magic and destroy them.

Their magic shields saved them. Ice attacks and mirror magic echoed his fire attack back at him. His shield cracked in some places. These people were the real threat of the army, not the easy pickings he dealt with earlier. The wind currents changed as the storm's power grew. Where they attacked him with wind and ice, he launched fire and landed by them to shake the earth back at them. Their ice bridge shattered and melted. Just as his own shield broke a hole near his front foot. A squadron of melee fighters barreled toward the hole with weapons charged with spells.

He roared in their direction and stepped closer to the river. Defending this spot would only last until their beast showed up. This location was the shallowest part of the river, where they would drain it to slow the skeljaskrimsli and let Vakandi to attack him. With the thick falling snow ruining visibility, Mx. Konst would not know when to pull the levers without some sort of signal. Fire met weapons and their clash of steel and scales sparked. With their hammers raised and swinging around on him, he swung his tail back. Hits landed on his foot, but he would not take flight. He resisted burning the forest too much until the beast arrived. He would not let the enemy gain another front on the battlefield.

The frigid waters, a mix of slush, crashed into his back shield, sending lightning like cracks all along it. They splintered and shattered apart when a boulder of ice flew into the shield. It hurt like a snowball into his neck, but it was no avalanche. He blasted fire in the direction the attack came from and took to flight before the Skelij fighters did more harm.

Up above, he saw them running straight to the city instead of to the main road. Snow flooded his vision as a deep laugh gurgled below him. The skeljaskrimsli lowered their head and silenced as they trudged down the river. The water only rose to its eyes, its back exposed in the shallow water. Vakandi roared a pillar of fire toward Vakfored, melting all the snow and evaporating the liquid. He did not waste any more energy on the signal and went to slow his enemy before they went too far. Vakfored had to take care of the Skelijs. The beasts would fight each other.

He landed right along the river, exposed and without a shield, like a city without a wall. Claws dug into the dirt and he threw the river mud ball at the monster. Fire would be futile with all the water, earth would ruin the river drain plans, and the wind would do little. He would not use life magic to this bringer of destruction either, he knew it thrived on life magic as much as himself. Magicless, he desperately flung another mud ball at the hard shell.

The river turned dark brown and bubbled furiously. The skeljaskrimsli's head exposed, its mouth agape, stomping on the ground, a suctioning sound as it snagged its claws in the deep mud. Not fast enough, the water levels lowered to be a meager stream for a moment. Vakandi blasted the beast with fireball after fireball. Steam rose off its shell as ice crept along its back. It quickly turned to mist from the ongoing barrage. Vakandi got closer and swiped at the skeljaskrimsli's head with his own sharp claws. It sounded the same as a blade and shield crashing into each other. The skeljaskrimsli's scales held while Vakandi's claws splintered. He still had three more sets of claws. Turning around, he risked exposing his back and whipped with his tail, aiming the strong plates to try crushing the scales on the beast. There was a chance the attack could be strong enough to flip the monster over to expose the soft abdomen.

The weight of the enemy countered as the sharp icicle teeth bit and held on the tail. Vakandi cried in pain as the teeth dug further into his flesh, its digging claws gripped on tighter too. He blasted a ball of fire at it, but it did nothing again but melt the surrounding snow. The beast latched on and laughed again through its stuffed mouth as the water from the river rose. The reservoirs below had filled already. Vakandi was losing all advantages fast.

Instead of calling on the wind to take flight, he prayed to the earth to save him. To keep him grounded and not in the river, to gift the strength he needed now. With a puff of smoke, he ran away from the river, wings flapping to push him forward more. Snow swirled around and the trees shook with his efforts.

The plan worked as the skeljaskrimsli cried at being pulled. It used its weight and dug its hind claws into the mucky Paondel River. Vakandi shifted his power and listened to the beating winds from his wings, and rose into the air. Within a single beat of a breath, he was up in the air. Before the skeljaskrimsli let go, he flicked his tail under him to launch the monster away from the river to expose its underbelly.

Which led it closer to Vakfored.

It landed on its side, legs kicking, and it screamed as fire tongues ate at it. He could not destroy a mythical beast like himself so easily. It rolled over to protect itself before Vakandi could finish them. Lowering its head, it charged toward the city. It ran over its own Skelij without concern, just in pure desperation to get to shelter. The Skelij did not stop, but followed its bloodbath wake. Greed filled their eyes at the easy target in front of them. Fifteen rings ripe for the picking, only a handful of meddlesome mercenaries to their remaining army.

Vakandi burned the oil pits in front of the mythical monster. It dug its claws into the ground like a till and pivoted around to avoid them. The army thinned and spread out, but grew more frantic as the Skelij approached their goal. Vakfored's fireworks shook the air upon detonating, slowing Vakandi down. The mercenaries outside of the city were retreating to go further in. Some Vakfored still meandered about, looking lost and confused.

If only there had been a shield, a wall to delay this onslaught.

A way to pierce the stomach of the skeljaskrimsli and burn it.

It got near, too large to go through the main road, but strong enough to raze the smaller houses. If it breached into the city, the army would destroy all the Vakfored within. It could make a simple path for all Vakfored to arrive at Engill's Perigon.

Vakandi Foreldri made the only wall he could, blasting a pillar of fire at the houses of the fifteenth ring right before the skeljaskrimsli made impact. The ring painted in oil, made of simple wood and stone materials, burst into flames straight up into the sky. The skeljaskrimsli did not stop, blinded with pain. It crushed the buildings while heading north, its progression slowing as it tried to get through. Vakandi flew ahead and toward the mountain, burning the fifteenth ring. Hatred for the monster hurting his hatchlings sunk deep to his core that it touched the essence of earth and trembled the land. It sensed his desire to slow the enemy. Houses toppled from the force while the fires rose. Making it become the wall to slay skeljaskrimsli and stop the Skelij army.

The skeljaskrimsli's body stopped as it hit the edge of Engill's Perigon park, burnt and destroyed. Its heart stopped. The wound it created in the city ran from the outer ring all the way to the tenth ring.

Vakandi's heavy heart forced him to chase the rest of the army out in a blind rage and away from his burning city.

21. DINNER

Sisal's hand let go of the dagger she held. It would not save her and did little to bring its normal comfort. There was nothing she could do with it at this point. Vakandi Foreldri's eyes were closed, his neck bent, and wings drooped. The light glistened off the water near his closed eyes.

She reached a hand out, but the normal words of comfort would not work. It was not her place to forgive his actions he did to an entire city. She was not an ambassador. Hearing his side of the story now made sense of how the outer ring burned. His fires destroyed a section of the fifteenth ring and parts of the fourteenth. A dark permanent crescent mark split by the Burnt Road that showed when the darkness set into the city of Vakfored.

"You signaled for the river to be drained and then used earth magic to slow the skeljaskrimsli down. You destroyed the city's wells and the fire piping system. The fire ate more than what you burned initially. My grandparents talk about how you did it on purpose to destroy the people who no longer listened to you. They lost friends there."

"I'm sorry. I know my words mean nothing, and I wish I could have

been stronger, could have prepared you more. That day I will never forget."

"You could have said sorry a thousand times by now. You should have."

The dragon flinched at her words as if she physically assaulted him. He kept silent, like he did for a century until this morning. His inaction was the easy option to avoid penance.

"Stop sulking and do something," she said. "At least saying sorry would have been an action. Something! Instead, you vanished into this cave and did nothing but glower down at the people below you."

One breath. Then two, and finally, the golden eyes of the beast opened up. "There was nothing I could do that would fix the past and help your future. But someone else could help with the present in order to prepare you, Sisal, for the future."

Sisal crossed her arms. The light from outside of the cave decreased. She could not waste time asking him to explain why he thought she could lead. "I am here for Vakfored's future. Sunset is now only an hour away. Are you sure there is no more to your story?" She had to record all of his stories the moment she returned to the city. The stories her grandparents told her were not wrong, but they were only on one side of the fire. Not the other up in the air stopping a scaled monster that crushed through the buildings. The fact it only got to the tenth ring was incredible. Her family made her think Vakandi turned his back on Vakfored. The skeljaskrimsli overpowered him. He did everything and even relied on the river to expose the monster.

"Do you at least regret never coming back to Vakfored?"

"Yes." He said it so firmly that she felt it through her bones. He continued, "What I'm saying has no meaning because of my silence since. I hated the taste of my flames when they burned the city. The smell that filled the air suffocated my heart worse than when the Black Forest would burn. I thought and revisited the past over and over in my mind how I should've put a shield over the rest of the buildings. The skeljaskrimsli attack left me drained of magic, bleeding, and with a broken tail. Worst of all, I hated what I did. I was the monster who attacked you. I went back to my cave, where hundreds of the vulnerable Vakforeds had already run away from. The children and King Kirrad rushed out to help put out the fires in the city. They ran all the way from my mountain to the city. I only drank my elixir and cried. So many people were orphans and homeless because of me."

"Then why should I let you go today?" The threat was there, but her emotion was not behind it.

"Because I have one last tale to tell. The one that led to you, Sisal."

Her heart skipped a beat. She sat down on a chair, looking up at him with empty hands, and ready to listen.

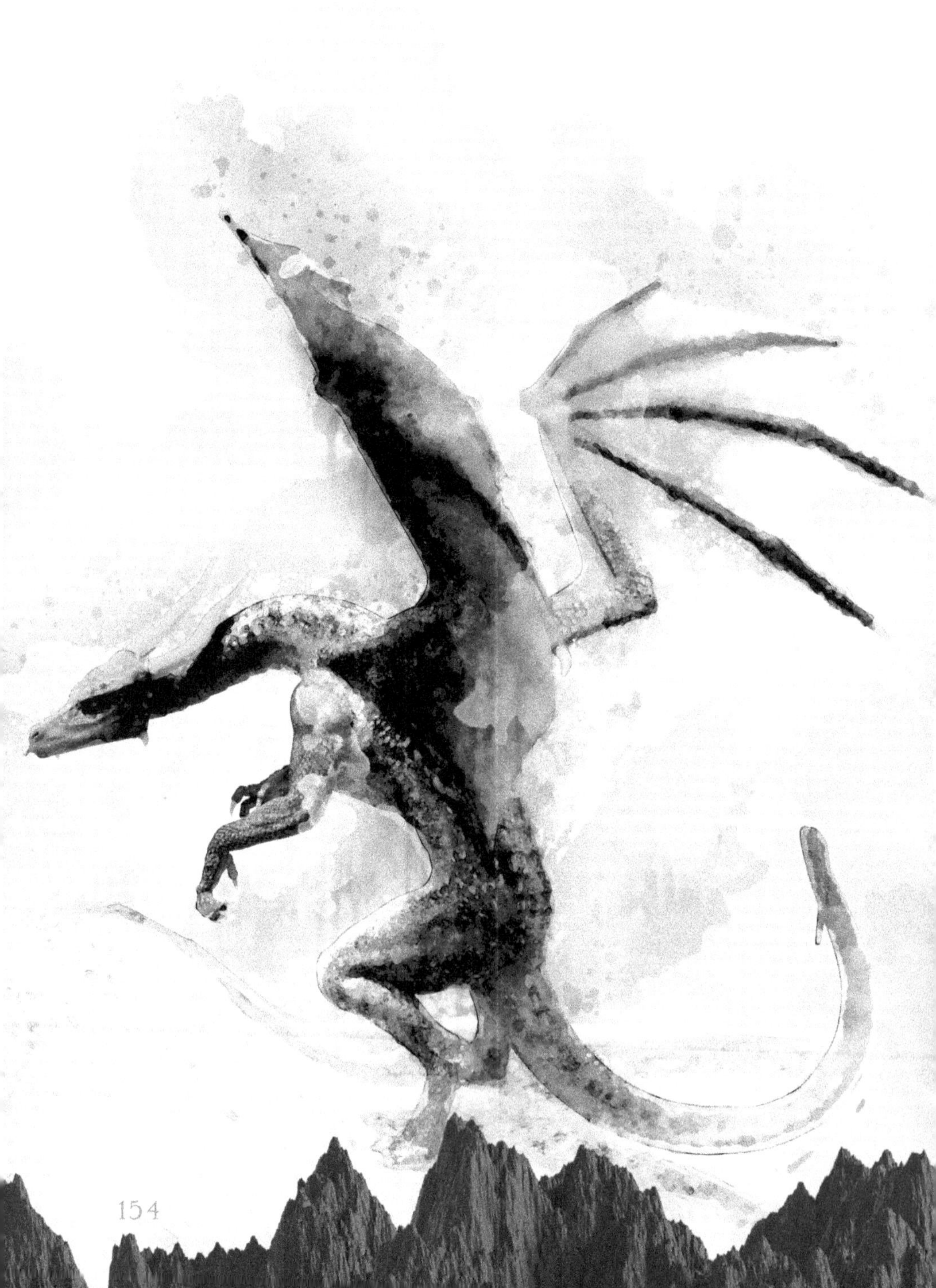

22. THE PICTURE FRAME

With the Skelij army gone, the city cried. It was the only way they knew how to recover. The city knew of death, but the War of the Beasts caused a complete shift in their world. They feared and shunned their music away. Their guardian once loved them for their art and use of magic. But now he burned them down and a new darkness settled in their hearts as the smoke, ash and snow covered their once colorful city.

Only one person kept going. Kennezben Konst the Third's hat tilted down to Vakandi, waiting for a greeting. Vakandi only puffed out a small bit of smoke before tucking his snout under his tail. The cave felt large and empty of all life. He always lived alone, but now even the gold felt cold.

"You aren't looking too sunny." The orc said after a while.

Vakandi grumbled back, pivoting to avoid looking at them. The orc only stepped around and placed a hand on Vakandi's dark ember red tail, near the pink skin where the Skeljaskrimsli removed his scales. The elixir sealed it up, but the scales would take time to repair.

"I'm here to collect my gold. I have a stipend to pay for the mercenaries who died, too."

"Fine. Take this pile." His tail smacked one medium size pile, coins

spilling down. "That will cover their deaths, funerals, pay the living as well, and give you a sum to live off on. Now go away."

They put a piece of paper across his tail. The numbers of the deaths and toll it cost of Vakandi's failed protection of Vakfored.

"I'll only take what you owe me. No bonus. I don't feel like robbing a dragon today."

"But another day?"

"Only if you have a contract." They crossed the cave and took an empty-looking bag off their back. With quick hands, he counted out the gold, making sure to not take extra.

"A contract?" Vakandi asked, worried about what it could mean. "Are the Skelij still causing problems?"

"No. They're all gone. It's what the city might still need."

"They need a better guardian." He tightened up in a ball again.

"They do. They need to create it themselves, though. King Kirrad is already gathering resources to build a wall of remembrance. Something able to withstand 'extreme fire attacks,' with the skeljaskrimsli scales as the base. He even wants one used on a door for that barracks." They pointed to the guest room for the people to stay the night. Now it was being named a barracks. From entertainment to defensive.

A wall of the past is not what he wanted, but they were predicting a prospective fate. The Vakfored were preparing for a future when a dragon would attack them. They feared him and what he would do to the next generations. He would never use his fires to hurt... he had thought that before. His hatchlings moved on to a new cycle, and he still wished to guide them. He could help set up quests for the city, huntings not as harmful as a skeljaskrimsli. Sending any monsters or people to attack Vakfored was the same as burning it down. He needed someone to help with this plan. "What do you think of acting as my agent?"

"No," They replied. "I hate that title. Call me an ambassador and we can talk." Their hand traced along the brim of their hat before going back to counting coins.

He unwrapped himself from his ball to talk. His hearth had burned out and his joints sore from the cold. "They are finally acting on the defense, and it's going to save them from me. If they are truly afraid of me, they will focus on protection as long as I stay unpredictable. For centuries, they saw me every week. Now I will hide here, hunting at night so they can't see me."

"I don't approve of this. It's only been two days. You can still repair the relationship. They will still love you with time."

"There would be that shadow of doubt in this current generation - and then it would vanish away with time and we would return to where we were before. Then what will be the next warring city or monster to attack? I could not handle the skeljaskrimsli without the reservoirs by the river. Given time, they will know how to destroy everything that comes near them." He did not feel happy saying the next words, so he pointed a claw at himself instead. "All the monsters."

Kennezben stopped counting coins and sealed the bag up. It looked the same as when he first arrived. Deep lines grew around his mouth and forehead. "The Vakfored are creators, and you want to change them?"

Already Mx. Konst the Third proving their worth. Vakandi thought about it. He did not want them to be greedy like other cities. He did not want to die, but needed some sign that the city could change, and mythical monsters like him were rare. How would he know the city had changed and be as strong as him if they never tried to stop him? He questioned his guest for the answer. "It seems I have grown too distant from the people, yet we need something more. What do you suggest?"

"All this gold and I can come up with an answer by the end of the week."

He pointed a claw at the pile near his guest. "That's all I have left. The rest belongs to the Golden Essence Bank."

Kennezben pursed their lips, resisting to show further emotion. "Well then, I have an answer now. You need to stop loving them, and

I can start erasing you from their history. I'll pay people to say hateful things about you in the tavern. Boo off the theatrical plays that talk of your noble actions. It won't be too hard since some people already grumble. I'll just be paying others to be louder. Make sure people remember the dragon of yesterday. Not the one from before when there were no adventurers, and you were the one who slayed the beasts."

The gold scattered again as he smacked his tail down next to the smaller pile. "You can do better. I want you to set up an official guild hall in the city to hunt monsters like the lich in the Black Forest. I'll guide you on upcoming threats and pay a bonus to you if it's a citizen of Vakfored. We will also give similar initiatives in another guild hall, one dedicated to the crafts where they will keep creating, but with a guided hand. Rebrand a wall and call it a picture frame that can't burn. Entrap their art, give them a canvas. Make a play that talks of the glory of the heroes like you in the battle."

Kennezben nodded, "Yes. Yes. It's brilliant, especially the play. Then we can even have them prepare more fireworks, with louder booms and color. Put up trade requests for various goods to be brought in, and keeping the two guilds separate, this would draw little attention. I will be the supreme master of both guilds, but guiding two other people who will have their names on the door. This will draw little attention."

"Sounds like I will need more gold."

"I'll leave that to you to figure out. But the lich is my first contract." They pulled out a magical quill and paper from his bag on his back. With a whispered word, the paper floated in the air as they wrote. "All right, let's first write the bylaws."

The Guild of Arts and Guild of Adventures were born that day. All making sure only Kennezben came to talk to Vakandi. The Guild of Adventurers would have to steal books and various arts that talked of Vakandi in praise. The Guild of Arts would replace it with talk of local fighters or distant heroes.

"I can't destroy the history of Vakandi without destroying you." Kennezben avoided writing the details of the first rogue quest.

"If the Guild of Adventures wishes to form a squadron to kill me. Then so be it."

They lowered their pen. "That's not fair. If they did that now, it's no different from a child throwing a tantrum to act out. They need to have time to make that decision. I'll figure out something to make sure it's only one brave and prepared soul if they do. You could be wrong though, they could attack my loud actors. They might still return to you with open arms."

His friend was only trying to warm Vakandi's soul. He hummed in response. They were not pushing him out of his cave. They listened to his opinion, and Vakandi would respectfully do the same. This friendly exchange of words reminded of his time with Bedruk, Lash, Helvin, and Engill. A conversation between peers, not like the ones he had with the Vakfored. His own hatchlings had grown and deserved to be respected. "I don't think they be foolish enough to only send one person after me when an army failed to kill me."

"The Vakfored have taught me that a flourishing speech filled with emotion can even convince anyone about anything."

"That was not too convincing. You will need more practice."

"I'll come by and keep trying. Only one pure soul can enter the cave."

If his heart still did not feel so heavy, he might have laughed. "Then how did you get in here?"

They pointed at their bag on their back. "I have a heart of gold."

Vakandi chuckled out a puff of smoke.

23. THE SUNSET DRAGON SCALE

"What happens next?" Sisal asked, following along Vakandi's slow walk to the cave's entrance. The soft yellow light of the evening sun greeted them. That story had been too short. She had to make him keep talking. "The War of Beasts was almost a hundred years ago. People have seen you flying out. Did you seriously choose this to make us hate you?"

"I needed to learn how to let go, and you hating me made it easier."

"That's not what you truly want! You wouldn't have coercion me into listening to your history of Vakfored. You want us to like you. I want to fix your relationship with us. Stay. We can plan something."

He reached the entrance and looked down at the city. The sun crossed his body, leaving him half in shadow and light. Growing up, seeing the dragon walk out of his cave used to cause her hatred and fear of the monster. Now she saw Vakandi as the tired, exhausted guardian who was done with their watch. Not even a hint of a smile stretched across his mouth.

"It is too late. You wisely made me swear on the magics. I think I would like to do one more flight over the city."

She placed a hand on his foot. "Wait. You are a powerful dragon, centuries of experience. There has to be a way out of the bargain."

"Sisal, I hear you. But it's not what the city wants. They want me gone."

"No! I got this mission from the Guild of Adventures. You said so yourself. You set up the quests and demands of the place."

A small trail of smoke rose in the air from his snout as he sighed, remembering everything. "Sorry, recalling Mx. Konst made me miss them again. Once they passed, we stopped creating quests. We rarely had to fabricate a quest in a long time. We had time to enjoy each other's company instead of working near their end. If you take out your mission details, you'll see that it's not from the Guild of Adventurers."

Sticking her hand into her bag, she willed for the contract paper to appear. The bag gave it to her. She unfolded it with shaking hands. The assignee had not been a signature, but the government seal of four chair members. The paper threatened to fly away as Vakandi Foreldri stretched out his wings. Quickly, she got a handhold on a scale and climbed up, tossing the mission paperwork on the ground. "You're taking me with you."

He laughed, making it harder to climb him, but he stayed still. "I can't believe this. After all this time, this is the first time I'm ever giving anyone a ride on my back."

Sisal settled in by the plate right before his neck, and held on tightly, not wanting the guardian—the protective parent of Vakfored to go away from her. "I tried earlier, but you shook me off."

"A peaceful ride."

"Please, no twists, twirls, or spins." She looked out at her home. The vast city and its fire proof defense and weapons. She wished she had packed a symbol or way to contact the city that Vakandi was a friend, not an enemy. "Put a shield on and fly high so they don't think of you as a threat."

The light rippled around them for a moment and she felt the magics knot together like it did around the barracks door, but acting as a net. His powerful wings lifted them up into the air. Nestled between his plates, she felt the currents flow by her sides. One hand out, the air coasted around her hand like it was a wing. Each beat of his kept them up in the air and the pink tinted clouds. It felt freeing being up here. The weights of the earth dropped away. To see everything, the guild halls, the bank, the gardens, the city, the wall, created a new perspective. The dark outline on the fifteenth ring truly created a picture frame look on the round city. People were signaling along the walls, aiming and waiting for him to come into range. Fortunately, he did not. The freshly turned farms prepared for seeds of what to come, hopeful for the right amount of rain. They had hope for the new season.

"I promise-" the wind washed out her voice. She cleared it to speak loud enough. "Shadow of my Sun!"

"No need to shout. I can hear you."

She grumbled, but did not want to lose her thought. "I will undo to you what you did to me. I'll plan for a future where you will be happy and welcomed back in Vakfored. Starting with the statue that I knocked over."

That statue was the size of her. It would look like a crumb from this high. Vakandi could have fixed it any time, but he wanted the people to stand on their own.

"That would undo everything. I can't be the guardian any more after the scar I left."

"We can't change the past. We can plan the future like we have planned for attacks. Now we will plan to invite you over."

He circled the outline of the city once before returning her back to the cave. The shadows growing longer as the curve of the sun lowered.

"It's up to you to tell the stories." Vakandi stated.

"Stop giving up!"

Gold easily bribed Kennezben. They should've pushed more if they really cared for Vakandi. Sisal agreed with one point. She had to make a flourishing speech right now. "We've created the impossible. We have mage scholars. They'll figure out something you have never thought of before. Don't doubt your Vakfored." She hugged his plate, the hard roughness leaving a light scratch on her face. "We should've said it before, but thank you for everything."

She held him there for a moment, his head lowered and she felt a pressure on her back. A fire dragon was warm. She did not want to let go. The oranges of the sky grouped next to the reds and the first twinkling stars of the night appeared out in the east where the bison roamed. Her heart wanted to stay here longer, but her mind knew that she had to push Vakandi away to save him.

"I will always love my Vakfored." His deep voice was stronger this close to his heart. "Thank you for hearing my apology." With a claw, he dug a small scale off near his chest, its deep red colors reflecting the setting sun as if it was on fire. "This is the last item I will give to you. 'In the circle of our lives, nothing binds you, even death.'"

He stated the motto of what it meant to be Vakfored, and he was their Giver of Life. She was the Giver of Death.

She hugged the scale and looked up at him. "I'll make that true about the magic that holds you to this promise."

He touched the scale as more stars slowly appeared. "I am certain you will. Goodbye Sisal of the Vakfored."

24. THE NIGHT

Listening to the tales all day took a toll on Sisal mentally and emotionally. She glanced around the cave. It was as large as the palace. With Vakandi in here, it felt comfortable. Now her footsteps echoed, especially now that she moved all the gold into her bag. She even found her bow buried under the gold. There was a receipt to return part of the gold to the Golden Essence. Some of it was for the Guild of Adventurers and Guild of Arts as the last bit of payment due, plus some interest. The rest she could keep, it would make her set for life and live a life of ease.

By the light of the baubles wrapped around the stalactites, she confirmed there were no more spiders in the barracks room, and that the window stayed shut. She got comfortable on the bed furthest away from the damaged door. Everyone knew Vakandi Foreldri left his cave. They didn't know if he would be back. She knew the truth. Even with these thoughts, she fell asleep in the defenseless cave. The rest was brief. The city knew she went up on this quest because of the sword ceremony the King did. They probably thought she was dead or too cowardly to do the mission. A nightmare of some greedy bandit coming in to ransack Vakandi's home jolted her awake. Forcing herself up out of the bed, she dragged her feet out to preserve a side of history.

Collecting the items which Vakandi left behind, each one a historical item that should belong to a museum. There were close to forty uncracked Bedruk Oresword pottery. She already packed the tapestry with the woven song in her bag. She collected the others. Her favorite was the one where he stood on guard over the city. She chuckled as she put on the necklace from the werelions attack. It would have been too small to be a ring for Vakandi. She secured the scale he gave her earlier. The spell book she pulled out to flip through it, stopping on the pages where it talked about the uses of a dragon scale.

There were descriptions on how to make sturdy armor, powerful weapons, and even a spell of telepathy. She was not a scholar of the magical arts, and she wanted to burn the book, but every side had a story. Even though Vakandi said it was not all factual, maybe there was a truth in there a peaceful mage could determine, like a way to undo the magics. That would be her first mission she would commission for at the Guild of Arts and the Guild of Adventures. Someone would find the answer or create it. She would make sure Vakfored learned the truth and loved Vakandi for all he did. Forgive him for the misunderstanding and create a new future for Vakfored.

She chortled at the thought of how even gold seemed to go in a cycle of passing hands. All this money and already she planned on moving it along for an important goal. Vakfored had its freedom and could stand on its own now that Vakandi left. They did not need to become a warring nation to take resources from others. She would make sure they would continue to trade, but have a militia ready to defend. She would create a new Guild, a Guild of Prosperity. Where the exchange of gold and items took their own cycle. Like these historical artifacts came back to Vakfored. She would make sure instruments and choreographers would come back to Vakfored with the return of music. A commission for the Guild of Arts to translate the woven fabric and return the music and songs of old. Right now, Vakandi and Vakfored were distant from each other, as if the dark had swallowed them and blinded them both.

Walking out of the cave, the stars twinkled in the west, but the yellow sun rose in the east like it always did, over the potters and baker kilns, near the mage tower. Every day it came back to start a new day, and a new cycle. "'In the circle of our lives, nothing binds you, even death.'" She repeated the saying. "I will make that true for you, Vakandi, our watchful parent."

The darkness of the war and anger with Vakandi Foreldri will end like the night did. Today started the first day for the Vakfored where they could breathe at last on their own.

THE END

If you enjoyed reading *The Sunset Sovereign: A Dragon's Memoir*, please rate it on the store you bought it from, post it on social media, and talk about it with your friends and Vakfored. An author is similar to a dragon in the fact we hoard all the praise we can get. Thank you.

VAKANDI AND THE CARDIGAN

Forward: This story takes place immediately after Chapter 7. The River. I wanted to show a scene were Vakandi had a chance to enjoy the chaos of the Vakfored and the joy they brought him, in more than a sentence.

***

No fire dragon would ever declare their cave stagnant or muggy. To them, that would be comfortable. The strongest dragons find caves in warm areas to avoid the waft of cool air. Other dragons loudly complain about their drafty cave every time they feel it, their joints stiffening and shivering from the temperature drop. Vakandi tucked himself into his second cavern, in a smoothed-out spot in the corner, and curled up. Every time he shivered from the bitter cold air, it caused the injury on his back to flare up. He grumbled in complaint and puffed out more hot air to fight back the frigid, icy spring day. He wanted to melt all the blasted snow. Seeing the white powder would warm him with embarrassment at recalling how he lost his temper at the Vakfored people. All because he failed to be there for them. To think that a great fire dragon like him would be stuck licking his wounds in the corner of his cold cave because of some—an actual mountain load—amount of snow smashed into his back.

This time his stomach gurgled as loud as his grumbling earlier. It had been days since he last ate. He could not go out and fly, or even walk, to hunt for food. Doing so would reopen the wound and it would need more time to heal. He glanced at the dark scab on his lower back, right above his tail. One of his precious plates was gone and he could not grow it back. It was also unlikely the scales would ever grow over the area. The ugly pink would always be there.

Feelings of pain, cold, hunger, embarrassed, and loneliness only made him spiral more. The best way to deal with spiraling emotions would be to fly above. And he couldn't even do that. Like all things in life, he would just have to wait until the status returned. If it was summer, he wouldn't be this miserable. He would sleep under the stars out by the foothills of the mountains. It would be warm, but then there would be no avalanches that could hurt his back in the first place.

He would still be foolish for getting angry at the Vakfored, who were simply venturing out to explore the world on their own.

Something crunched the snow outside by the first cave's entrance. It sounded like a group of things that were louder than the mountain goats that would foolishly hop on by, like a popping snack for him. Most thieves that came after the Golden Essence's gold were quiet and would not risk breaking-in days after a snowstorm. He forced himself up, grimacing at the aches, and crept out of his warmer cave to the front where the small gold piles sat. He paused and positioned himself beneath the roof's low point, which acted as a divider between the two caves. The slight amount of sunlight was a welcome relief, as it prevented him from hitting his head. By the time he got to the first cave, he saw seventeen people that closely resembled icicles marching into his home. Ice coated their hair and clothes while clumps of snow surrounded their feet after their hike from Vakfored to his home. The snowstorm was four days ago. The previous day was when they finished Vakandi out of the avalanche. They must have left immediately to get here.

He looked back behind the cave and noticed a lack of items. Every time he landed in the inner ring of the city, they gifted him something. Bedruk offered a lot of bowls only people could use. So many that Lash made a crate to make it easier and safer for Vakandi to carry all the pottery. Gifting the Vakfored a Bedruk bowl now would end up being like he returned the gift, and that was rude. Vakandi's papa at least taught him that much.

The people finished shuffling in, past the bank's gold and near Vakandi. Some took off their hats and scarves, others started removing their large packs on their backs. A couple of donkeys complained about being dragged inside an alpha predator's home. Vakandi's mouth drooled at the sight of the animal, but he backed up. Those donkeys were not for him, no matter how much his stomach grumbled.

Engill put her hands on her hips and raised her voice to him. The bags under eyes were easier to notice on her human flesh. "Get back into that cave now. You need to rest. I can smell the blood in the air below the..." She politely stopped herself. "You'll get a chill and a cold from coming out in your weak state."

Vakandi puffed out a bit of air and inhaled it back. He stuck his tongue out in disgust before sucking it in to hide it as well. His breath was rancid and needed some evergreen trees to brush up. Embarrassed, he shuffled backward to his warmer cave. It seemed the people had the same idea of finding warmth. A few people deposited gold from their backpacks and the packs the donkeys hauled in the first cave. The bank's piles were growing.

"I stay warm by using my fire to heat this cave," Vakandi said.

"Keeping your blood in will, too." She pointed to a corner. "Sit there and we will start treatment right away."

"It will heal on its own."

"And you will get an infection."

He laughed as he settled into the corner. Even with his scuffling, the spry older woman kept up with a speed walk next to him. "Dragons don't get infections. Or even a cold."

She pointed to the corner. "Settle down. Let's keep that fact true."

Slowly, he settled down, curling his tail again. The wound still stung. He watched as the people gathered in, removing their packs in various places. They did not sit on the floor, instead they began pointing to various spots in the cave. While they ran around with a string, took notes, and argued about chairs and tables. Engill climbed up on Vakandi's back to inspect the wound.

When the Vakfored arrived on the first day, they disrupted the silence and brooding in Vakandi's life, and his smile grew as he heard them bicker.

"We realized we don't visit your cave much beyond depositing gold. With everything you've done for us, we wanted to help you in return. Any complaints?" Engill asked.

She asked a broad question that instantly became narrowed as she scraped at his back. He turned and growled. She smiled at him with a tiny knife in her hand. "Ah, so it does hurt. It's swollen because of an infection. You focus on them while I remove the bad flesh. Ginger!" She shouted.

It was not the root she shouted for. A young woman still bundled up in her hiking equipment approached. Her hair weaved into a braid stuck out below her woven hat. "What? We just got here. Can't we rest for a moment?"

"Sickness doesn't stop because you take a nap," Engill lectured.

"I heard you tell the Shadow of the Sun rest is needed." The woman replied.

She responded with such fire that she should have been named Pepper.

"Do you even want to learn?" Engill asked.

"As much as you want to debate. What is it you need? We shouldn't be bothering his rest like this."

Vakandi cleared his throat and feigned interest in the chalk lines being drawn on the slate wall across from him. Already a human and orc worked together to drill a hole in the wall. Vakandi had seen them make paintings on the wall, but the drilling was new. Maybe the art would be more dimensional this way. A dwarf was pulling out a chopping axe and pointing to the outside.

Before he could question what they were doing, Engill patted his back. "So, what do you think? Are you alright with that?"

He widened his eyes as if it would help him hear the past better. Ginger had her arms crossed, but smiled. The body language of people was never helpful. The kind spoken woman, Engill, had her head tilted, still holding that knife near his injury. He had no clue what they said. He directed his voice to Engill. "I would like to hear your opinion on the matter."

With a reassuring smile, she gave it. "I'm not versed in these plants she talks about. My central focus is about the plants readily available in the Black Forest."

Vakandi involuntarily constricted his muscles. He could easily burn the forest down, but that didn't stop the death within it. It would only help it grow. The people did a better job pushing it out slowly than he ever did. Engill was still standing on top and noticed his twitch. She patted his scales and said, "I won't be using the plants directly on you. With your permission, I will clean your back and use the samples to test to see if I have purified the plants enough to be used on you."

"While she wastes her time on that," Ginger pointed to a large backpack and continued talking, "I plan to actually use living typed plants to find medicine for you."

"I appreciate the gesture." Vakandi said, "But I will be fine. I just need time."

"You'll suffer pointlessly," Ginger declared.

At the same time, Engill softly said, "Listen to us, Shadow of my Sun."

Ginger waved, signaling Engill to talk. The older woman graciously bowed her head. "This was not a minor injury. There are talks of powerful medicine out in the world that can heal instantly. With how you protected us, we want to find this in case you get hurt again."

"Even a big, powerful dragon can use some help." Ginger said. Other Vakfored nodded in agreement.

A loud thwack sound came from outside of the cave. Its sound echoed in the caves. A few more happened in succession. The sound of an axe chopping a tree down. Vakandi rarely had to deal with multiple interruptions like this. A dwarf started pulling out a massive amount of purple yarn from their packs. It must deal with the art they were going to do on the wall. The guild master of the woodsmen had come over to help. Vakandi ignored the tree cutting and focused on Engill and Ginger. "Vakfored, you always create. Who am I to say no to your innovation? I would greatly appreciate if you find a way to speed up my healing. But I don't want my blood leaving this chamber."

Ginger snorted. "You lost a lot out in the snow."

"What my apprentice should say is that you can trust us, and we will respect your wishes."

"Then feel free to research using the samples as explained, but please keep me informed." He turned his head back to Ginger, getting a crick in his neck for switching back and forth. "I'm curious to know what plants you've brought? I know of a few key magical essences that can aid in magical healing."

The rhythmic axe cutting stopped as the cracking sound of the tree falling brought further attention again. Vakandi could only imagine the plume of snow rising from the tree's impact to the ground. He could no longer ignore the fifteen other people who shuffled around his home and inquired. "What are you doing?"

The orc who was drilling in the wall came up to him. "It's darn cold in here. We're going to be staying a while until those two," he nodded up at Engill and Ginger, "finish researching a healing draft for you. I want to be warm and comfortable."

"How does drilling into my cave help with that?"

The human who was coring another spot stopped. "Sun of my Shadow, remember the water pipe? We want to give you one. That's going to be an extensive project, too. But we can't have the pipes freeze, so first we are making a fireplace."

For the first time, Vakandi learned how to tsk his tongue. "I want to make sure I understand. You are building a fire dragon... a fireplace?"

"Aye," the human replied. "You said so yourself. You use your own breath to keep warm here. We want you comfortable."

He lost his words. Centuries of meditation on the ways of the world and he had nothing to say about having a fireplace besides what his mum told him to say. "Thank you."

Granted, those words only applied to other dragons, and he was certain there was a lesson about avoiding people at all costs. If he listened to all her lessons, he would have missed out on seeing the city grow. They blustered about in his cave, dragging wood in and cutting it, hammering away to the point it gave him a headache, hearing and feeling the earth shake at their onslaught. Even Ginger and Engill could not stay calm for a moment as they argued the most effective method to work in the area. Everyone was setting up stations. Work orders were quickly being made about needing a table and chairs. The access to water would speed things up too. These unexpected guests were going to be here for more than a few days with all the items they packed. They had packed only dried meat, fruits, and hardtack. Engill was the only one to bring in the death plants and their tincture.

He avoided twitching too much from Engill's cutting, but kept a close eye on her. Until someone pushed a giant yarn collection next to him. The deep purple belonged on berries, not near Vakandi. The dwarf and a human guild master of the woodsmen smiled up. "Shadow of our Sun," spoke the guild master, "this man saw your pain and suffering the other day and wants to bring you more comfort in this unbearable winter."

He put a hand on the companion. The dwarf stroked the yarn in his hand like it was his beard. "I understand how the joints hurt with the cold. I couldn't imagine the massive amount of pain your injury is bringing. Don't want to, to be honest."

Vakandi puffed some smoke out at that remark. "Tell me then, what is it you have in mind to make it comfortable? It seems you Vakfored are running about the place."

A mighty dragon letting the small ones roam around. The situation was joyful. He was finally like that orc who cared lovingly for their child days before. He was a parent in the chaos.

The dwarf gestured towards the yarn and expressed, "I wish to fashion for you something my grandma constructed for snowy days. A cardigan."

The vocabulary of the people always befuddled Vakandi. He learned the word armor had a broad term. It could mean a helm or greaves, or both of them at once. Although a shirt protected people from the weather and exposure, they did not consider the items as armor. The people were scaleless, but they were small enough to always mingle like this in each other's homes.

"Enlightening me? What is a cardigan?"

The dwarf undid his jacket, and stretched out the soft, flimsy, looking garment underneath that weaved around in design and knots, golden buttons standing out on the red. "This!"

He noticed small holes in the knitted cardigan, which made it impossible to keep a person or a dragon warm.

"I guess it could be comfortable." Vakandi did not want to chase away the people, especially when they were being so forward with their kindness. But a dragon doesn't wear clothing. "Do you even have enough materials? You only recently started the looms." He nodded toward the Woodsmen guild master. "Plus, didn't I mention you should use the fabric for your people-"

A tickle on his back paw, between the claws, caused him to snort suddenly. Looking back, Engill and Ginger giggled.

"Oh my, a dragon is ticklish here? What a weakness. Maybe you should–cover it up gratefully." Engill said.

Vakandi quickly lost his funny bone. That was the voice his mum used to give him. "You know what you're doing." He said to correct the previous statement.

"Of course!" The dwarf was unchallenged. "I should introduce myself. I'm Jokran, and with these needles, I will make you comfortable and ease your pain."

Vakandi felt embarrassed for trying to turn away from the help. This did not differ from when Bedruk started offering all the clay pots. Vakandi never wanted them initially, but now he treasured them more because his friend was gone. A fireplace to remember and cherish other visitors, a place for them to stay and visit for a bit, and Vakandi could host them! Having winter armor to keep the chill off would make visiting the city easier. It would allow him to see his domain glisten when covered with snow.

"I look forward to seeing what you can do." He said with joy.

Even more donkeys bayed at the entrance as they resisted being dragged inside. Vakandi, though, could not get up to investigate, and he felt uneasy about that. The cheering and applauding of his people diminished his stress of invaders quickly. He really needed a break from being on edge around them. Things were fine.

More people settled in, along with more gold and yarn. They brought along other companions. A human brought a cat and her freshly born kittens. The human did not want to leave them alone at home. She bundled up the fur covered creatures in a box. The felines mewed and scattered about the moment they were free in Vakandi's cave. Such tiny little creatures he easily ignored. They could enjoy the various pests of the cave. The people seemed amused by their antics as they dashed about. One bravely cried up to Vakandi, protesting at the dragon for taking the best warm spot. The mother nuzzled near him, bringing the rest of the litter nearby. He reminded himself it was only a few more creatures to the disorder of his cave. This was the noise of the city slowly entering his home. He grinned and rested his head near the cat. Both their tails twitching as they watched the people run about with their work orders.

The Vakfored had sucked the air out of the bags to decrease the volume of the yarn. This idea intrigued Vakandi, and they talked about how to create infinite bag space. Engill contributed a lot, and Ginger would provide a counterargument. Jokran worried that the yarn would become knotted up–or all of it would appear instantly. Fortunately, solving this problem would not happen instantly. The Vakfored were visiting for a while. Days passed and the pain in his heart and back vanished with time under the constant attention of everyone.

He did not understand how the people kept laughing at the kittens. They would try to climb on everything and would get in the way. The cats seemed so smug, like they knew and ran the place. One even swatted at Vakandi to threaten him into moving. Ginger giggled and picked up what she deemed "a tabby" away from the scared dragon. He did not feel fear. He just wanted to snap at the creature and had to resist for the people's sake.

Jokran made progress on the knitting and explained to Vakandi how the stitches worked to weave together and make various designs. During summer, some rows of the cardigan had to be undone. Jokran's girlfriend came over to help with the project as the fall colors appeared. Vakandi, Jokran, and his girlfriend would sit near the edge of the cave looking out at the red, orange, and yellow leaves that lined the mountain and valley near the Vakfored. The giant ball of yarn was slowly shrinking and the last of the shoulder braids were being stitched together under gentle hands. Ginger and Engill had helped heal Vakandi's back and made progress on a potion they called the Dragon's Elixir. It would only work to make barrels of it at a time, and Vakandi really liked its golden color. Other people stayed and slept, their various sounds of snoring echoing through the night almost as loud as their tools during the day. The fireplace hearth took shape and so did the tables for everyone.

The kittens grew into small cats. They had not yet returned home, apparently thinking the cave was theirs. Vakandi was at first fine with them, but they kept attacking Jokran's yarn. One skein ran down the mountainside, causing it to get snagged and stained. Everyone laughed, even Jokran. The people were just happy to have the time together, and if they had to spend more because of dirty yarn, so be it. Vakandi learned from them again how to be patient, and not worry about the end of their brief lives.

Right when the first frost appeared, Jokran wove the loose ends of the cardigan into place. Vakandi's back ached with the cold. Before he could moan or complain, the Vakfored brought wood into the cave along with food. They prepared fireworks on the outside of the cave. Vakandi lit the fire with a single puff, and the flame spread out quickly along the wall. Laughter filled the room and people handed glasses of water around from the now working pipes. Cool fresh water was refreshing after all the hard work. A line connecting the city to the dragon's home. The scraping of chairs echoed through the room, intermingling with the rhythmic beats of dancing feet and the booming sound of fireworks outside.

All the noise and bustle making his own heart flutter with excitement as Jokran brought over the finished purple cardigan. He could not do it alone, and like always, the city of Vakfored grouped up together to solve a problem. People of all ages lifted or used magic to carry the heavy piece of clothing to Vakandi. He could not help but beam looking at the cardigan. This was a ceremony, and he joined in on the celebration. Jokran knitted the cardigan in this room. It was not a surprise. Vakandi could easily walk over and grab it. A few times, he touched it to feel its softness. Now, as the magic lifted it into the air, he felt like a young hatchling ready to take flight. His wings stretched out, and the holes lined up as the winter armor slid onto his back. Next to his claws, on each side of his shoulders, sat an extremely long roped cord, and an equally paired short one. Vakandi was not sure about the fashion taste or that the cats whacked at them like they were toys. The pets mowed and chased after the dangling cords.

Jokran chased off the cats on one side, while Ginger picked up the tabby on the other. "Shadow of our Sun, pull the short cords!"

Without hesitating, Vakandi listened. The holes around his wings tightened up, leaving room for him to fly. The long cloth draped down to his tail resting nicely along his neck. It even had three buttons to seal up along his stomach with a bit of magic. He jiggled about, pulled a bit again on the cords, feeling how they tightened and loosened. With a satisfied sigh, he looked at Jokran to tell him, "This is quite cozy and warm. Thank you."

ALSO BY LAURA HUIE

The Thedre Trilogy

When she learns her home isn't Earth, she will do anything, even take on the gods, to belong there.

Book 1: The Unchosen

Fire spells her name. Dreams whisper of a lost magic…

Book 2: The Astray Chosen

They both need to find the gods. He, to save the country. Her, to kill them.

www.ingramcontent.com/pod-product-compliance
Lightning Source LLC
Chambersburg PA
CBHW070544310726
48982CB00010B/1467/J

* 9 7 9 8 2 1 8 5 3 4 3 7 0 *